SUN
YOUR BACK

'There is a field somewhere beyond all doubt
and wrongdoing. I'll meet you there.'

Rumi

Naira Khan

DESTINY MOTIF
PUBLICATIONS

Destiny Motif Publications (destinymotif.com)

Facebook: @nairakhanauthor

Ordering information:
For details, contact : destinymotif@outlook.com

Print ISBN: 978-1-8384278-0-1
eBook ISBN: 978-1-8384278-1-8

Artwork by Katharina Leighton
Cover design by Saskia Sevenster
Typesetting by Raspberry Creative Type
Proofreading by Helen Bleck Editorial Services

Author's Note

Writing this novel was a labour of love and a professional healing. I am a psychologist who specialised in working with children and their families in Zimbabwe before moving to the UK. My work progressed to research in sexual violence and development of intervention programs to improve the system where children report abuse. However, one cannot work in this area for long periods. It takes an emotional toll on psyche. The faces of the women and children and their stories stay with you.

This book does contain some upsetting incidents of sexual and domestic violence. Should you find these incidents difficult to deal with, please talk to someone appropriate who will help you to understand your feelings. You could contact your GP or a counsellor. I have outlined some resources below.

My intention is not to upset anyone but to honour women and children who have suffered abuse and survived – and those who have died. It is hoped that the lives of the characters in this book help others to better understand the problems survivors of abuse face emotionally and with their relationships. For the rest, let us be more aware and empower our children to protect themselves.

This is a prayer for a world where women and children live free from violence.

Naira Khan

RESOURCES

Zimbabwe
Domestic Violence: Musasa Project.
Telephone: +(04)706152/706284 (Harare)
Childline Zimbabwe: Telephone: +263 732116116

South Africa
POWA (People Opposing Woman Abuse).
Telephone: +27 11 642 4345/6
Teddy Bear Foundation.
Telephone: +27 11 484 4554

UK
Women's Aid: helpline@womensaid.org.uk

Acknowledgements

This story was enhanced by invaluable support from many people. Their advice and support has been pivotal in developing Diara's story:

In the initial development stages, I am grateful to Rosie Whitehouse, Paul Serjeant, Howard Sargeant and Joan Serjeant. Thanks to Susan McKenna for a fabulous weekend where we workshopped the development of the characters.

To my beta readers:

- In the UK: Hugh Serjeant, Susan Mckenna and Susan Stephens
- In South Africa: Shehnilla Mohamed, Suzanne Leighton, Fiona Baxter and Susan van Breda
- In Zimbabwe: Kwadzanai Nyanungo and Shaheena Karbanee

Crucial legal advice came from:

- Nabilla Abdulla, Acting Principal Policy Officer, Queensland Department of Justice and Attorney General, Australia.
- In Zimbabwe: Brighton Pabwe, Legal Practitioner

To Liz Treacher, for her expert advice on self-publishing.

To my editor, Jane Hammett, for all her hard work and advice. Priceless.

1

LONDON, 2007

The shrill sound of her mobile ringing penetrated her sleep. At first, Diara assumed it was her alarm. She lay still for a minute, waiting for consciousness to fight its way to the surface and the alarm to ring again. She wondered why she felt so tired; she usually woke ten minutes before her alarm began to ring. As she stretched and sat up in bed, the ringing began again. Diara leant over and retrieved her phone from the bedside table. The alarm stopped again. She sat up in bed and shivered, wondering why it was so dark on this cold February morning. She pressed her mobile to switch off her alarm and only then realised that she had three missed calls. Unknown number. And it was 2.35 a.m.

Diara was still in the process of absorbing this when her mobile rang again. She answered immediately, her heart beating faster.

'Hello?'

'Dee? Diara?'

Diara recognised her sister, calling from Zimbabwe. Her unease escalated, making her sleep-laden voice rougher than she intended when she responded. 'Shaan? What's wrong?' Diara sat up and swung her legs out of bed. Dimly, in the back of her mind, she realised that it was only two hours later in Zimbabwe. The caller, her older sister Shaan, was

1

not in the habit of calling so early in the morning. In fact, she didn't call at all. It was Diara who called home once a week. Her chest tightened, and she began to wheeze – her usual symptom of anxiety.

Shaan was sobbing. Great big gulps.

'Shaan, what's wrong? Where is Mum?'

'Dee, can you come?'

What had happened? Nothing good was going to come out of this conversation. Shaan's sobbing had escalated again. Diara got out of bed, slipped her feet into her warm winter slippers and walked over to the window. The radiator was cold. She wanted to give her sister a moment to calm down. She was gripped by fear. What was Shaan going to tell her? A weight pressed down on her chest as various scenarios flitted through her mind. She tried again.

'Hold on, Shaan. Catch your breath and tell me what's going on … slowly. Is it Mum?'

The sobbing continued. Diara waited. She tried to steady her breathing. Cleared her throat to stop the wheeze. She forced herself to remain silent. While she waited, she tried to collect her thoughts. Something must have happened to Mum. Or maybe one of the girls. Maybe Mum was ill? As possibilities tumbled through her mind, finally, after what seemed like an eternity, Shaan spoke again.

'Dee, please can you come? I'm not sure what to do.'

'Do about what?'

Diara's fear blossomed into terror. Something terrible had happened. That was obvious. Shaan couldn't speak; she was gasping and sobbing.

'Where's Mum, Shaan? Put her on the phone.'

No response.

'*Shaan! What the hell is going on?*' Diara felt hysteria rise in her. But her shout had the desired effect. After a few more sobs, Shaan gulped.

'The police took Mum, Dee.'

Diara froze. She felt perspiration on her upper lip and in her armpits. 'What do you mean, "took Mum"?'

The sobbing returned. But Diara had lost all patience. 'Shaan! What the hell! Tell me what is going on.'

Finally she got the information she needed. And it was not one of the many scenarios that had passed through her mind.

'Dad's dead, Dee!' Shaan gasped.

Diara was appalled. Her silence grew.

Shaan's voice rose two octaves to a screech. 'Come home, Dee. We have to bury Dad. He's dead.'

'How?'

'Mum ... um ...'

'What?'

'Mum said she killed him.'

2
ZIMBABWE, 1995

Mandy made her way along the dreary, silent corridors of Ward 12 – the ward for those whose injuries were psychological, unable to be seen. The ward was in an annexe outside the main hospital. The hospital board explained the separation as providing a 'quiet, serene and peaceful area' to help patients recover. Perhaps. More likely, they wanted to separate the crazies from everyone else. That had always been Mandy's opinion. The stigma of mental ill-health was as strong as ever.

Mandy was a clinical psychologist, employed by the medical school of the University of Zimbabwe in the Department of Psychiatry. As well as teaching medical students about the nuances of mental health and behavioural science, Mandy was required to assist with patients who had been admitted to the hospital, then follow up with them more at her weekly outpatient clinic.

Mandida, meaning 'you love me' – or Dr Kaputa, as she was known at the hospital – was a proud African woman who honoured her heritage by not interfering with her naturally curly hair. It was twisted into dreadlocks that came to well past her shoulders and swayed as she walked towards the nurses' station. She was also blessed with a face that often broke into a smile and had a calm, happy

4

demeanour to match. Her perfect white teeth were admired by many. She wore navy blue trousers and a white shirt with long, loose sleeves and buttons down the front. Her ears were adorned with silver discs the size of an old penny, with a small moulded elephant attached to the top of the disc, as if it was walking along the rim.

'Hi, Sister. How are you?' Mandy smiled at the nurse sitting writing notes in a book.

'Dr Mandy! I'm happy to see you!' replied the elderly Sister in charge of the annexe.

'It's always good to see you. I'm here to see Diara Kruger.'

Sister Mariga's smile disappeared, replaced by a grimace. 'Well, you can try but I must warn you that her mother was here earlier and they had some sort of disagreement. The child was upset – when I got there, she was weeping profusely. Mrs Kruger appeared to be shouting at her. I had no choice but to ask her mother to leave.'

'Hmm. What was Mum saying to her?'

'I didn't hear much. I only heard Mama saying, "Is that what you want?" The child was so distressed, I had to intervene.' As she talked, Sister Mariga spoke quicker, and her voice rose.

'You did the right thing.'

'I hope so,' she said. 'I did not like Mama's body language – it was almost threatening. I tried to speak with the girl after Mama left, but she would not say a word. Just wept.'

'Okay. Let me try,' Mandy said, smiling. 'Maybe she will talk to me. Don't worry – she probably just needs time.'

'Room four,' Sister Mariga said, smiling back.

Mandy squeezed the Sister's shoulder and made her way down the corridor to the left of the nurses' station. This was the section that housed patients who required extra vigilance. She did not like to think of it as the suicide-watch corner.

Mandy stopped at the small nurses' station, strategically placed with a view of all four rooms in the corridor. The young nurse at the station smiled in greeting but continued talking quietly on the telephone. Mandy peered into room four from where she stood. All the rooms had glass windows that covered almost half of the wall. This allowed nurses to keep an eye on them from the nurses' station. The girl lying in bed on her back had her eyes tightly shut. It was obvious that she had been crying, and still was. She periodically used the back of her hand to wipe away tears. She was a brunette with thick, straight hair that almost touched her waist. Her long fringe was pushed to one side and her olive skin was very tanned. Her legs and arms looked almost emaciated.

Mandy made her way to room four and tapped on the glass wall. The patient quickly rubbed her eyes and looked over to the door. Mandy saw that she had almond-shaped eyes with tawny irises. Her nose was short and straight, and she had the kind of full lips that women paid thousands to emulate.

'Hello, Diara,' Mandy said, smiling and making her way to the bedside. 'I'm Mandida Kaputa and I am the psychologist in charge of your case. May I sit?' Mandy sat down on one of the two visitors' chairs in the room. 'How are you feeling?'

'Tired. Sleepy ...' Diara's eyes welled up again.

Mandy nodded and remained silent to allow Diara to collect herself. She busied herself studying the file notes. She dated the sheet and prepared to take notes of any conversation they had. She did not think it would amount to much. The patient was agitated, and she moved around constantly in bed. Her hands were fisted, bunching the pale cotton blanket. She was chewing her bottom lip. She exuded an air of fragility, and Mandy felt an urge to lean across and hug her. To reassure her.

'How's school? Are you enjoying your subjects this year?'

A small smile appeared on Diara's face and she nodded.

'Yes. I am doing my O levels and want to study the sciences next year.'

'Do you have any special friends at school?'

'Yes. Leanne McKenzie. She's been my friend since grade one.'

'You've been friends since grade one?' Mandy asked with surprise, trying to steer the conversation to happier topics.

Diara nodded. 'I sometimes spend the weekend at her house. Those are really fun weekends.'

Mandy noted that Diara was relaxing as she talked about her friend.

'I bet you tell each other secrets.'

Diara tensed up again.

'Did you speak to Leanne about whatever was troubling you?'

Diara's face clouded over, and she shook her head.

'I thought we could talk a little about why you are here in hospital. Are you up to it?'

Diara nodded very reluctantly. She sat up straighter in bed and waited for Mandy to speak.

'The file notes say that your mother called an ambulance as she had found you unconscious. You had taken many painkillers. Is that correct?'

Diara avoided eye contact with Mandy and nodded.

'Did you know that they were painkillers?'

Another nod.

'Did you have a pain anywhere? A headache? Or some other pain in your body that you wanted to go away?'

A shake of the head.

'So, why did you take the pills? Was something troubling you?'

The girl looked away. For perhaps twenty seconds, Mandy looked at the back of the girl's head, her luxuriant black hair, her olive neck. Mandy had made the opening approach. The girl had replied. That was a start. A good one. The rest would have to wait.

'We all have pain in our minds sometimes. I'm sorry yours was so strong that it made you want to take those pills. I'd like to talk more about it sometime so I can help the pain go away. But I can see that things have been difficult for you. So, rest now. We'll talk again later, if you like.'

Diara's eyes welled with tears again. She looked down at the blanket and nodded.

'That's fine, Diara. You don't have to say anything today. Just rest and get stronger. We will meet and talk a few times before you return home, and after that—'

'I am not going back there!' Diara's face was contorted with distress.

'Back where?'

'I'm not going back home!'

'May I ask why?'

'I'm just not going back there. I hate it there. If you send me back there, I will find another way to leave again. Please, I can't go back!'

'Look, Diara, I really want to help, but you have to give me more information so I can understand what the issues are. I must have a good reason to move you out of your present home. Is anyone hurting you? Are you in any danger?'

Diara stared off into the distance. Her face took on a determined look as her eyes focused on Mandy. 'I just can't stay there.'

'Diara, there's something I should have mentioned earlier. Whatever you share with me will remain with me. You can tell me anything you want, and the law tells me that I cannot say anything to anyone – not even your parents – without your permission. You are in control.'

There was no response but more weeping.

'Okay, why don't you rest now? I will come back tomorrow, and we can talk some more, then decide what to do. Hopefully, you will be feeling stronger tomorrow.'

Diara nodded and lay back. As Mandy turned to leave, she noticed that Diara's eyes were shut and fresh tears leaked out.

Mandida left the room and made her way back to the nurses' station to write a summary of her initial meeting with her patient. While immersed in this task, she was interrupted by the sound of footsteps running down the passage towards her. It was a teenage girl, frantically looking around. She ignored Mandida and peered into each room until she found who she was looking for. Mandy watched her run into Diara's room and touch her shoulder. She was lying on her side, her back to the door. Diara turned. When she realised who her visitor was, she sat up and they embraced. Diara's face was contorted with pain and it was obvious that her friend was sobbing too, by the heaving of her shoulders. Mandida watched sadly as the two girls held each other. The visitor tried to soothe Diara by smoothing her hair and making calming noises. Diara was sobbing, sounding almost animalistic.

Mandida recognised her desolation and desperation. It was very painful to witness. She shook her head and admonished herself. 'You are no good to her unless you keep your head, Mandida.'

❂❂❂

Mandy went back to her office and rang Sophia Kruger, Diara's mother. She thought it might be a way to access more information about her client before their next meeting.

'Has anything happened to Diara? Is she all right?' Mrs Kruger asked.

Mandy detected concern in her query. 'She is as well as can be expected, but I am concerned about her.'

Silence.

'Mrs Kruger?'

'Why? What has she said?'

'Well … not much, I'm afraid. She is very fragile. I was wondering if I could meet with you and Mr Kruger. Perhaps together we can come up with some strategies.'

There was another silence. Mandy frowned. It seemed strange that Diara's mother was asking these questions, when her teenage daughter had just tried to kill herself.

'Mrs Kruger, I am concerned about Diara. Why did she feel the need to express her anxiety in the way that she did?'

'Um, I don't know. Can we talk about that next week?' Mrs Kruger sounded hesitant.

'We can, but I need to know whether this has ever happened before, Mrs Kruger.'

Mrs Kruger's South African accent became more pronounced. 'No, no, of course not! I think she just forgot how many pills she had taken. She has really bad period pains, you know.'

Mandy remained silent, rather than respond to Mrs Kruger's ludicrous statement.

'We can't see you this week … André is so busy at work. You know what, let me speak to him when he gets home and I will ring you back.'

Reluctantly, Mandy agreed. But her gut feeling, that there was so much more to this story, grew. She suspected that Mrs Kruger had a hidden agenda. Mandy picked up her file and made her way to the hospital social worker's office, one floor below.

Mandy knocked and stuck her head in. Kudzai Khumalo was at her desk, frowning and scribbling furiously on a piece of paper. 'Hey, Mandy, come in. I need a break. The universe is plotting to stop me completing these maternity leave forms!' She threw her pen down and pushed herself up from her desk. Kudzai was fifteen weeks into her second pregnancy. She came over to Mandy and the women embraced.

'Come and sit down and tell me what's making you frown.' Kudzai walked over to a caramel-coloured three-seater couch in the corner of her office that looked as if it had seen better days. She plonked herself down, leant back and stretched her legs out in front of her with a sigh of relief. 'Having babies is hard work, my dear.'

'But you make it look so effortless! You are flourishing.'

'I'm fine, but I will be glad when this baby is born.'

'Kudzai, I wanted to discuss a case, if you have a minute.' Mandy sat in a matching chair opposite the social worker.

'Of course. What's up?'

'I have a fifteen-year-old girl in the ward. Her mother found her unconscious after she apparently overdosed on pain meds. I have just been to see her. She won't talk much about what happened, but she insists that she won't go back home.'

'Is there a boyfriend that her parents disapprove of? Have you spoken to them?'

'Well, that's the thing. I'm not getting a good feeling from them. The mother was observed speaking to my patient in a threatening manner this morning – Sister had to intervene. I just called the mother, asking her to come in with her husband, and she said she would let me know. Let me tell you, Kudzai, something's not right. I feel it in my gut.'

'Hmm, there is probably more to it. So, what do you want to do?'

'I was thinking, could we make a home visit? Legally, only the social worker or the police can make home visits. I was hoping I could tag along with you. Is that okay?'

'It should be fine. I can see why you're concerned. If a minor is refusing to go home, that is a point to investigate. Furthermore, if parents are reluctant to come in, that's another red flag. Most importantly, if my child swallowed a load of pills, I would like to know why, and I'd want to know how I could stop it happening again.'

'I'm not sure if they're in denial but genuinely concerned, or confused, hurt and with no idea what to do. But somehow, I'm not getting that feeling from this situation. Like I said, I think there's more to it.'

'Well, let's see if there is. When would you like to go?'

'Can we just show up?'

'Not usually, but in this case, we probably should.'

'Let's go now, Kudzai.'

Mandy saw the surprise on Kudzai's face, and explained quickly. 'I know it's after four, but if we went now, we would probably be able to meet both husband and wife. I think that will help us understand the situation, and Diara, better. She's not talking. She's fearful. She does not want to go home. She's hiding something.'

'Okay.' Kudzai picked up her bag. 'Let me get the relevant paperwork and clear it with the boss to avoid any problems.' She grimaced.

'Good idea. I'll do the same and meet you in the foyer in fifteen minutes.'

✪✪✪

'So, what's our game plan?' asked Kudzai as they drove down Sherwood Drive during rush hour. The family lived in Meyrick Park, near Sherwood golf course. Meyrick Park was the affluent part of Mabelreign, a suburb to the west of Harare. Most of the homes had been built for young families and had three or four bedrooms and over an acre of land. All the houses they passed had large front gardens. A few of the gardens were loved and looked after, but the majority were neglected. The houses were fenced or walled, as was customary in Harare. However, this could not detract from the beauty of the trees lining the roads. The flame trees – or flamboyants – were a magnificent sight. Their flowers were deep red and velvety. The appearance of these bright red blossoms was always a sign that Christmas was near. Flamboyants had no scent, but still butterflies and small birds flocked to them.

'Basically, we are concerned that their daughter tried to kill herself. Do they have any idea why? Any relevant history? Any relevant relationships? Has it happened before?'

'Good idea,' said Kudzai as she spotted 22B Anzac Road and turned into the drive. A scruffy, undernourished black Labrador was visible through the bars of the closed gate. He was sitting quietly in the drive but leapt up when he saw their car and began to bark.

Mandy hooted and they waited. After a few minutes, she hooted again. A woman walked towards them from the back of the house. She was a large woman, probably in her mid-fifties. A white cotton headscarf was wrapped around her head and she wore a white apron over a printed cotton dress. Was she the housekeeper?

She unlocked the large padlock securing the gate. Kudzai and Mandy got out of the car and walked towards her. Kudzai greeted her respectfully in Shona, the local dialect, calling her Ambuya. Grandmother. She explained that they had come from the hospital to see Mrs Kruger about Diara.

13

When she heard Diara's name, the elderly lady began to shake her head rapidly and covered her mouth with her hand in horror.

'How is Ms Diara?' she asked in English. She then lapsed into her mother tongue, telling the women how worried she had been about Diara. Mandy and Kudzai nodded and listened patiently. After a few minutes, Kudzai again asked to see Mrs Kruger.

'Go to the front door. I will go inside and open it.' With that, she hurried off towards the back of the house. Mandida and Kudzai made their way to the front door. The house was painted a salmon colour and had a red-tiled roof. There was an empty swimming pool in the front garden. It had cracked due to being exposed to the elements with no water to protect it. The garden was dry, invaded by weeds, and untidy. The wooden front door was battered, its paint peeling.

The door opened. Ambuya stood there. With her was a girl who looked about twelve or thirteen. She was tall, with an athletic frame, and was wearing brown shorts and a white T-shirt – probably the PE kit of the school she attended. She was a paler version of Diara. Her shoulder-length blonde hair was pulled back into a ponytail, and she was looking at them with a mixture of curiosity and fear.

'Hello. I'm Mandida, and this is Kudzai.' Mandy smiled and held out her hand in greeting.

'Who are you?'

The girl reluctantly touched the hand Mandy held out. 'Annika,' she said. 'Annika Kruger.'

'Hi, Annika. We wanted to see your mum. Is she here?'

'Mum's lying down. She has a migraine. Are you the police?'

'No, we are not,' Mandy reassured her. 'We're from the hospital. I am sorry to hear your mum is not well. Is your dad home?'

'No, he's at work.'

'What time will he be back?'

'Um, I'm not sure.'

'Do you mind if we wait?' asked Kudzai.

'I don't know when Dad will be home.' Her gaze darted to the gate and back repeatedly.

'Can you come back tomorrow? There is no one here, only me and Amaani. Shaan, my big sister, is at work.'

'I understand. Maybe you can check on your mother, see if she's awake?'

Annika hesitated then with great reluctance turned and walked away, into a room to the left of the entrance hall.

Ambuya beckoned them in. The room was bare apart from a few pairs of shoes lying near the entrance to a passage leading off the hall. Straight opposite the front door was a seating area, lower down from the hallway. The room was furnished with drab overstuffed sofas, a television and a sound system with a turntable. Glass doors led out to a veranda. Some rusty white garden chairs and a table were visible through the glass doors. Like the front, the back garden – a large piece of land – was bone dry. There was what appeared to be an orchard at the far end. The house and garden were surrounded by a concrete wall that was at least five foot high.

Ambuya gestured for them to sit. Mandy noticed that the house was spotless – probably due to Ambuya's efforts. Ten minutes passed. They waited for someone to appear. Ambuya had disappeared. Eventually a car horn sounded. The hooting lasted for a minute or so, stopped briefly then began again. In the house, sound and movement were restored.

They heard activity from the section of the house where Annika had disappeared to earlier. There were footsteps, and suddenly she appeared again, followed closely by a younger girl.

'Mum is still sleeping. You had better go because my father is home now. He does not like it when people come!' Annika spoke quickly, her fingers playing nervously with her skirt. The younger child stood a little behind her, holding Annika's hand and sucking her finger. She stared curiously at the guests.

'It's fine, Annika.' Mandy spoke reassuringly. 'We would like to meet your dad.'

Annika and the younger girl turned and disappeared into the house. After a few seconds, a door banged shut.

Almost simultaneously, the front door opened. A big man was silhouetted in the doorway. It was difficult to distinguish his features as the light was behind him. It was well after five thirty and the sun was beginning to set.

'Yes? Who are you? Can I help you?'

André Kruger took a step forward. Mandy saw his sun-baked complexion, the dirt under his fingernails, the dusty *veltskoens* on his feet. He wore khaki shorts and a misshapen white T-shirt with a Coca-Cola slogan on it.

'Is somebody hurt?' He seemed unperturbed. Relaxed.

Kudzai stood up and walked over to André.

'Good afternoon, Mr Kruger. My name is Kudzai Khumalo. This is my colleague Mandida Kaputa. We work at the hospital and are here to discuss your daughter, Diara.'

Mandy saw Kudzai put her hand out and then stop.

André's demeanour changed, and he looked wary. 'To discuss her?' The corners of his mouth turned fractionally upwards. The ghost of a smile.

Mandy glanced at Kudzai, whose hands were plucking at her cardigan, arranging it over herself.

'Why? What's she said?'

'Well, not much,' said Mandy. 'We were hoping that you and Mrs Kruger could help us understand why Diara would take such a drastic step.'

'Because she is stupid and ungrateful,' André responded. 'Anyway, we will deal with her when she comes home.'

'Well, that's just it, Mr Kruger. Diara refuses to come back home. Would you know why that is?'

'How the hell would I know what goes on in that mind of hers? She's the hoity-toity one. Full of airs and graces. Thinks she's too good for us. I cannot hope to understand the mind of a woman.'

Mandy wiped a bead of sweat from her throat. 'Child.'

'What?'

'She's a child. Your daughter.'

André Kruger's blue eyes narrowed.

Mandy was having to dig deep to find her inner, non-reactive psychologist. 'Mr Kruger, in my experience, a child does not do what Diara did because she feels she is superior to everyone she knows. She is troubled by something, and we are trying to find out what, so we can help her.'

Kruger did not react well to Mandy's chilled tones. Mandy saw him stiffen. His fingers were curled tightly around his keys and his eyes flashed with anger. 'Really, Madam?' he said in a sarcastic voice. 'What gives you the bloody right to come into my house?'

'Sir, legally we have every right to conduct a home visit for a patient who is in distress,' Kudzai informed him, a fixed smile on her face. 'Now if you don't mind, we would like to meet Mrs Kruger before we leave.'

André Kruger looked startled. Unfamiliar territory for him. He fixed Mandy with his cold blue eyes, then looked past her towards the back of the house. 'Sophia!' he bellowed, keeping his eyes on Mandy and Kudzai.

The three of them remained frozen in place: Mandy seated, Kudzai and André standing, he glaring and she staring off into the distance.

After a few minutes, the lights came on in the hallway and sitting area. As their eyes were adjusting, a woman appeared and stood near André. 'Ja, André.'

The first thing that struck Mandy about Sophia was the difference in age between her and her husband. She was probably in her early thirties, by Mandy's estimation, whereas André was on the wrong side of forty-five, or maybe fifty. She was also a foot shorter than her husband. She had a delicate frame and was wearing a scruffy pink cotton dressing gown. On her head was a black scarf, tied in the fashion customary to Muslim women. It was Diara, but older, her face riddled with pain. She looked at the guests impassively. Sophia Kruger had some Asian heritage. That would explain the children's unusual names. As Sophia lifted her hand to tuck an errant strand of hair into her scarf, Mandy noticed an angry red scar on the inside of her wrist.

Mandy got up and held out her hand. 'Hello, Mrs Kruger. I'm Mandida Kaputa. I spoke to you earlier. This is Kudzai Khumalo, the medical social worker at the hospital.'

❀❀❀

Limply, Sophia shook Mandy's hand. Her gaze darted to her husband then back to Mandy. 'I am sorry I could not come see you today, but I have a terrible headache.' She too spoke with a pronounced accent, indicating her origins were in South Africa. But her voice was soft.

'I understand.' Mandy realised that the hospital visit would never happen if André had his way.

'We wanted to speak to you both about Diara.'

'Of course. But if you don't mind, I really am not feeling well today. I will ring you tomorrow and we will both come in to see you.'

Mandy looked at Kudzai, who nodded and spoke sternly to the couple. 'Please consider your daughter's well-being as a matter of urgency. We would hate to make recommendations without consulting you and your husband.'

'Of course, of course, I understand. Don't we, André?' Sophia spoke too quickly, and did not look at her husband or wait for his response. 'Thank you for coming, and for what you are doing for Diara.'

Mandy got the impression that they were being rushed out, and that Sophia was used to playing this role.

André walked over to open the front door as a silent invitation for them to leave. He did not respond to their goodbyes, just banged the door behind them then locked it.

'Well, well, well,' said Kudzai as they drove away.

'Something's not right, Kudzai. I have a gut feeling about this.'

'My advice? Listen to your gut.'

3

ZIMBABWE, 2007

Diara yawned. She had tried to sleep on the plane, but without success. Maybe her happy place would help, she thought, but no. Her mind was in turmoil, going over everything that had happened. She wanted to think things through before she got home. The next week would be a nightmare. *At last I'm going home to bury my father – but Mum. Why now, after all this time?* She had put up with Dad's abusive, alcoholic rages for years, so what had happened? It was hard for Diara to reconcile the idea of her timid, nervous mother with that of the woman who had beat her husband to death with a lamp. Where had that vicious streak come from? How had Mum gone from a fearful wife to a murderer? God. Maybe she'd just reached the end of her tether. You do hear about women who put up with abuse for years then snap. She sighed. She was too close to the situation. And she didn't know how she felt – about either parent.

She cringed inwardly when she recalled the look of pity on her boss's face when she had asked for a week's leave. She had considered not telling her boss why, but had opted for full disclosure. She imagined what her boss was thinking: 'Now I understand Diara better. That's why she studied psychology and why she works for an organisation that promotes zero tolerance for violence against children. Her own family is crazy!'

Accepting a cup of tea from the flight attendant, she dug in her handbag for the cheese sandwich she had bought at Gatwick. With her earphones in place and Cat Stevens' 'Peace Train' playing on her iPod, she leant back and allowed her mind to wander. She saw herself, as a child, walking into the kitchen after school and finding Mum sitting at the table, a cooling cup of tea in front of her. Mum turned around at the sound of Diara's greeting, and Diara stopped short at the state of her mother's face. It was swollen and bruised, and her lip was torn. There was dried blood under her left ear, which was partially covered by her headscarf. Diara felt tears roll down her cheeks, just like the ones she had shed that day in the kitchen. Sophia had attempted a smile but failed, as her hand went to her bloody lip in pain. Her loosely wrapped scarf came undone, exposing her earlobe. Diara gasped at the sight. Her mum's earlobe was split, and it didn't take a brain surgeon to realise that her mother's gold hooped earring had been ripped from her ear. She could still hear her mother's voice. *He pulled out my earring to sell it for beer. My mother gave them to me on my wedding day. They were my ouma's.* Diara shook her head to dislodge the memory, wiped her cheeks and concentrated on what she'd have to do in Harare. Mum would need a lawyer. Funeral arrangements for her father. She had to think about the girls. What would happen to them? At least they had the family home – her sisters would not be out on the street. With all these thoughts racing around in her mind, Diara finally dozed off for the final few hours of the journey. She only woke when the cabin lights were switched on.

Diara pulled her overnight bag behind her as she made her way out of the arrivals hall at Harare International Airport. The flight had taken ten hours and twenty-five minutes. No stops. No entertainment. Bad food.

As she made her way out of the terminal building, all her senses were assaulted. The heat was intense, even at seven-thirty in the morning. The sun was so blinding that Dee had to shade her eyes. The smell of perspiration hung heavy in the air. The arrivals hall was packed with large groups waiting to see loved ones. Diara had been one of the first people out past customs and immigration, as she had squashed all her possessions into her cabin baggage. The other passengers waited patiently for their luggage to arrive. She turned around to look at the airport building. She had forgotten how beautiful it was. Inspired by the ruins of Great Zimbabwe, it was a majestic white stone tower. The ruins were famous in sub-Saharan Africa: they consisted of millions of stones balanced perfectly on top of each other. The mystery was that no mortar had been used. The architect who had designed the airport had captured the beauty of the eleventh-century structure, the remains of a city where gold and ivory had been bartered with Arab and Portuguese traders.

'Diara!'

She turned around. Shaan was running towards her. She threw herself at Diara, sobbing uncontrollably. The sisters hugged for a long while. Shaan's weeping escalated; after a few minutes Diara was forced to pull back and take control.

'Come on, Shaan. Where's the car?'

Shaan pointed in the direction of the short-term car park across the road. Diara grabbed her by the arm and crossed the road, pulling her case behind her. In the car park, Diara repeated the question. 'Where's the car, Shaan?'

Shaan pointed down one of the six rows of the car park. Diara started to walk down the row, looking for the battered white Datsun 1200 which had been the family car for almost a decade. Shaan followed her, still distraught. They were attracting interest. They must look ridiculous, thought Diara, as she gratefully spotted the car and took the key from Shaan to open the driver's door.

Diara unlocked the boot and lifted her case into it, along with her handbag. She remembered that it was risky to leave any bags or luggage on the seats or on one's lap – this increased the chances of a smash and grab while stopped at any of the numerous traffic lights on the way to the city centre. Such attacks were common in Zim.

The sisters sat in silence as Diara navigated her way out of the airport. As she finally turned the car onto the main road, she allowed herself to be irritated by her sister's distress. Shaan was still weeping while she gazed out of the window. Diara did not engage with her sister, instead leaving her to calm down. It was incomprehensible to her that anyone could shed a tear for that brute. They were finally free of him. It had taken only one blow to get rid of a man who had wielded such power over five women. She thought about her training in human behaviour. It gave no clues to why her father had behaved as he did.

Any similarities between the two women ended with their surname. Diara's physical appearance was a combination of their parents' heritage, but Shaan looked like their father. She had curly, light brown hair that was scraped back into a ponytail. Her features were regular, and she had brown eyes that always looked uneasy. Today her face was red and her eyes swollen. Shaan seemed to be badly affected by having been first on the scene of the tragedy, Diara thought, taking the exit for the city centre.

Glancing at her, she noted the endearing gap between Shaan's two front teeth. The sight made her heart twist.

Now she was forced to concentrate on the road, which was gridlocked with cars, bicycles, vendors pushing carts piled with fruit to sell, and the notorious commuter minibuses. The latter, also known as *kombis*, were used by most people in Harare as their main form of transport. One *kombi* cut in front of her to avoid a pothole. Its driver then decided to circumvent the queue of commuters crawling down the road by mounting the pavement and cutting in front of traffic when the pavement ended. Diara slammed on the brakes to avoid a pedestrian running out in front of her car, narrowly missing a cyclist.

They were stuck in traffic for fifteen minutes. While they waited, there was a commotion on the opposite side of the road. Two minibus drivers were hurling abuse at each other. One had tried to cut in front of the other and had landed in a pothole, which had resulted in damage to one wheel. The passengers in the precariously tilted minibus looked terrified. There were at least fifteen people crammed into the minibus, which was meant to seat nine.

Finally, Diara was able to turn onto a quieter road which would lead her towards the western suburbs of Harare. Glancing at her sister, she noted that her sobbing had stopped, replaced by a fixed stare.

The road out of the city was lined with jacaranda trees in full bloom. Diara found no joy in the beautiful blooms, which cloaked the city in a purple mist come October. The blooms marked the end of the dry winter and the hope of rain in the summer. She looked straight ahead and tried to shut them out of her line of vision. However, no matter how hard she tried, the fragrance from the purple trumpet-shaped blooms infiltrated her nostrils, making her want to gag. She shook her head to erase her memories of the event triggered by the sight and smell of the flowers. She glanced at her sister, who looked calmer. Maybe now was a better time to talk to her. 'So, what happened, Shaan?' Diara asked softly. 'Why would Mum do that – now? After all this time?'

'I don't know. I don't know what to say.' Shaan took a deep breath, blew her nose, and began to talk. 'We were all asleep. He was out at the local *shabeen* drinking – and whatever else he does there. I woke because I heard him shouting and Mum screaming. I listened for a few minutes, hoping that it would stop and they would settle, but his shouting just got louder and louder.' Shaan stopped and wiped her cheeks with the back of her hand. 'I got out of bed and walked down the passage to their room. I could hear him slapping Mum. She was screaming. As I got to the door, I heard a loud thump, like something had been dropped, and then it was quiet.' Shaan stopped talking as emotion overcame her.

Diara waited for her sister to continue, negotiating the morning traffic. 'And then?'

'I opened the door. Dad was lying on his front, not moving. There was blood on his head, and blood was all over the floor.' She was talking rapidly, her voice rising. 'He had been sick as well – there was vomit on the floor near him.'

'Where was Mum?'

'Mum was there, standing near him, just staring at him. And on the floor was the lamp from her bedside table.'

'You mean the one made of malachite? The carved one?'

'Ja. The police took it away as evidence, because there was blood and bits of Dad's skull on it.'

'Who called the police?'

'Ambuya. Mum told me to fetch her. I had locked the bedroom door behind me because I didn't want the girls coming in, but when we got back to the room, the door was open and the girls were in there, upset and confused. Mum told Ambuya to call the police.'

'If it had been up to me, I would have buried him in the garden and told no one. Bastard!'

'Mum kept saying that he was trying to strangle her.'

'I'm sure he was,' said Diara dryly.

'Mum's neck was red because he had been strangling her with his belt. There was blood all over her face from her mouth. Her nose was bleeding. Her eyes were swollen and almost shut.'

The sisters were silent as Diara turned off Sherwood Drive onto Anzac Road, where the family home was located. Diara sounded the horn, and almost immediately Ambuya opened the gate. She had obviously been on the lookout for the car. Diara drove in and parked near the front door. As she got out of the car, Ambuya threw herself at her, wailing. '*Maiwe! Maiwe!* Missy Dee! Our father is gone! He has gone to our Lord!'

Again, Diara found herself in a situation where she had to pretend sympathy. What was wrong with these people? She felt as if she was in a parallel universe. Her father had been a shit. She would not waste any tears on him.

'Sorry, Ambuya,' she said, putting her arm around the distressed lady. 'I am worried about Mum. She will need all the help we can give her.'

'Yes, Deedee,' said Ambuya, using her mother's pet name for her. 'The devil came into her and took her sense away.'

More likely, gave her some sense, Diara thought, but kept her thought to herself. She turned to greet her younger sisters, who had come bounding out of the front door.

'Hi, Mum. How are you? Are they treating you okay?'
Diara asked her mother, hugging her. She was in the remand
section of Chikurubi Prison in north Harare, along with
other prisoners awaiting trial. Diara noticed that her
mother was carrying her prayer beads and automatically
moving her fingers along them, even while talking. Her
face and neck were still badly bruised, and her left eye
was bloodshot.

'Ja, I'm okay, Deedee,' her mother replied in her soft
voice.

'How are you?'

They sat at the small table in the common room used
for family visits. A guard stood nearby. Diara tried not to
look around. The smell of boiled cabbage was difficult to
ignore – probably from the prison kitchen. She tried not
to think about the conditions in the cells. The prison
authorities had applied to Child First, the organisation for
which Diara worked, for funding for children living in
prison with their mothers. Diara had been sent to the prison
to assess the children's needs and to confirm that funding
was needed. She recalled overcrowded cells and poor
sanitary conditions. It was usual for up to fifteen inmates
to be housed in cells of only about thirty square metres.

'What do you get to eat?'

'Well, there is maize meal three times a day. You know I
am not a fan of maize meal. The food has no salt or sugar.'

'What? Maize meal on its own?'

'No … um, there is kale or beans with it.'

'So when do you get meat?'

'The meat is not halal, so I don't eat it. The food is bad,
but the other ladies are kind. I must not complain. God is
good to me.'

Diara decided it was best to ignore her mother's last words, or she was likely to blow a blood vessel.

'Look, Mum, I brought you some meat pies and there is hot tea in the flask. Please eat.'

Sophia pounced on the offerings. She took huge bites of the pie and closed her eyes as she sipped the tea.

Diara gulped back her tears at the sight of her starving mother clad in the plain khaki prison shift dress. Diara had brought her a blanket and some dry food supplies, including biltong. She knew from her official visit that conditions at the prison were harsh – inadequate meals, no medication, cold cells.

'How are you?' Sophia asked again, still munching a pie.

'I'm good, Mum.'

'When did you arrive?'

'This morning.'

'You must be tired.'

Diara did not think she could continue the superficial conversation for much longer. She noted that her mum was not wearing her headscarf. It had probably been taken away in case she used it to self-harm. Her hair was long, braided and twisted into a knot. It lacked its usual shine, and there were many more white strands than the last time she'd seen her.

'I'm fine, Mum. I am going to see a lawyer for you tomorrow. Leanne recommended someone she knows.'

Sophia smiled vaguely, as if Diara had suggested purchasing a different brand of rice. Diara waited a few minutes for Sophia to comment but when nothing was forthcoming, she continued. 'Mum, did you give the police a statement?'

'Hmm? Yes. I told them that I hit André on the head with a lamp. I didn't think I had hit him hard.' Then suddenly, as if she had just realised what her daughter meant, she said, 'I don't need a lawyer, Diara. I already told them I did it. Why do I need a lawyer? They just have to ask the judge how long I should be punished for.'

Diara was exasperated, but she tried to be patient and calm. Why should Sophia know about lawyers? Her life had been sheltered, and she had no understanding of the law and its processes. It wasn't surprising that she thought her statement would be enough. André had tried to disempower her as much as possible.

'Because Dad died, you will have to go to court. The judge will hear all the evidence, then decide on a sentence.'

Her mum was silent as she digested this information, worrying her prayer beads. Diara sighed and decided to ask some more about the incident. 'Mum, how did you manage to hit him on the head? Dad was so much taller than you.'

For a minute, Sophia looked blank. Then she began talking rapidly. 'He was so drunk. You know what he's like. He was shouting and banging. He wanted me to get up and rub his back. I had a bad headache, so I told him no. He started to beat me. I tried to run away but he caught me with his belt around my neck and pulled me behind him like a dog. He was saying terrible things. Calling me terrible names.' Sophia stopped to catch her breath. Her hands were in her lap and her prayer beads were forgotten. 'He let go of me for a minute because he needed to vomit. So I grabbed the lamp and hit him. I just wanted him to stop. I didn't want him to die.'

'Of course you didn't,' said Diara soothingly. 'Don't worry, Mum, we will get through this. But it's important that you tell your lawyer everything that you went through with Dad. Everything he did to you.'

Sophia looked horrified. She muttered as she played with her prayer beads. 'Your father was a good man. He tried his best to look after us. Yes, sometimes he got cross and lost his temper. But I was the one who did things wrong.

I wasn't careful enough when I cooked his food, or when I did other things wrong. I made him angry.'

Diara was speechless with anger. She stared at her mother with disbelief. 'Mum! He was a crazy fucked-up bastard! Were you not living in the same house as us?'

'Diara!' Sophia looked shocked. 'You should not speak of your father like that. God will punish you.'

'No, Mum. God won't punish me for speaking the truth. You need to do that too – tell the truth. It's the only way that you will be allowed to come home soon.'

❁❁❁

Diara parked on Union Avenue in downtown Harare. As soon as she got out, several street children surrounded her. 'Hey, Miss! Miss! I can look after your car. Trust me! Only one dollar!'

It was a hot day. Diara quickly chose a boy to protect the car, then stepped into the cool interior of Takura House, where she signed the visitors' book. Behind the front desk was a sleepy, bored security person. He gave Diara a visitor's card to pin on her dress and pointed to the lifts that would take her to the sixth floor, where the law offices of Robinson, Gillmar and Mapfumo were located.

Leanne had urged Diara to hire Rudo Shava, a junior partner at the firm. Diara had a vague recollection of Rudo from university, where she had met her a few times when she had been out with Leanne. Rudo was a few years older and had been doing a postgraduate degree in law at the time. Leanne and Rudo's parents lived on the same street and went to the same church, so it was not unusual for the girls to bump into Rudo at the local shops.

'Diara, in Zimbabwe, or anywhere in fact, you need the right lawyer to represent your mother as an individual,' her childhood friend had urged her last night on the telephone. 'Rudo understands the issues around domestic violence – and its consequences for women and children. You need someone like that, or there is a great danger that your mum will be portrayed as a crazy woman who plotted to kill the father of her children. Rudo is progressive – she has taken some pivotal human rights test cases to the high court.'

Diara agreed that she could not choose a better lawyer to defend her mum. She had been impressed by Rudo before. Back in 2003, when she had still been working at the Child First Office in Zimbabwe, Rudo had applied to the organisation for funding for a survey on sexual harassment of women in the workplace. It had been Diara's responsibilty to assess grant applications, and although her main remit was to support organisations that raised awareness of, and tried to prevent, sexual violence against children, she had been impressed by Rudo's application. It was outside her mandate, but she had racked her brain for a week, reading and rereading the proposal to work out how it could fit Child First's brief.

That brief was tough – their research in Zimbabwe had found that one in three girls and one in five boys reported being sexually abused before the age of eighteen. The issues were overwhelming.

Finally, she thought of a solution, which she presented to her boss.

'Let's give them some money – a one-off grant – to do the research. We can justify it by recognising that sexual harassment is rife in workplaces. Same issues, different environment. It is disrespect of women. Our interest is in the effects of this hostile environment on children at home.'

Her boss raised her eyebrows. Diara pressed on.

'Look, it's ground-breaking research in Zimbabwe. It's not been done before. It will look so good in our annual report. Let's say that our grant is dependent on whether they can find a partner who can take forward any recommendations from the research: for example, a partner to fund legal interventions to change the labour law to include sexual harassment as a workplace issue.'

Finally, Diara's persistence – and her boss's political agenda – won. Money was allocated to the research. Child First's partners found additional funding from a German organisation that specialised in labour issues. And Diara contracted Rudo Shava to write the legal recommendations based on the research. So she was confident in Rudo's ability to defend her mum. It was everything else that she was worried about.

An elderly lady, who she assumed was Rudo's secretary, escorted her from the reception area down a passage and through a door that had Rudo's name on it, into a small office.

'Please take a seat. Ms Shava will be with you shortly. She's just on a call.'

Diara sat and waited. The window in the office gave a fabulous view of Harare city centre. Diara could see Africa Unity Square. Pre-independence, this square was known as Cecil Square after Cecil John Rhodes, the Englishman who had founded and named Rhodesia, the precursor to Zimbabwe.

The square comprised beautiful gardens and cooling water fountains. Again, Diara was confronted by the purple jacaranda trees. She tried to concentrate instead on the mesmerising sight of the red flamboyant trees in full bloom. People who worked in the offices nearby were sitting on the many benches in the square, enjoying the sun during their lunch hour.

A few minutes later, a door leading off the office flew open and Rudo entered. 'Hi, Diara. How are you?'

They embraced.

'I am so sorry about your mum. Sit,' said Rudo, shutting the door behind her. 'Would you like a drink? Tea? Coffee? Water?'

Diara accepted the offer of water and looked around the office while Rudo asked her secretary to bring the water. Rudo's office was spacious. A large desk strewn with files and a computer was strategically placed in the centre of the room.

Rudo came over and sat opposite Diara. She was smartly dressed in a tight black pencil skirt and white long-sleeved shirt. She wore high black court shoes and pearl studs in her ears. Her hair was in its natural state, cut close to her head in an elegant afro.

'You and your sisters must be devastated,' Rudo said. 'It's a lot to deal with.'

'Yes, it is. I met the officer in charge of the case. He wasn't sure when the medical examiner will be able to release my father's body for burial. I would like to have the funeral before I go back to London. I don't want the girls to have to deal with it on their own.'

Rudo made some notes in the file she had carried with her from her desk. 'Is that Sergeant Musekiwa? I spoke with him this morning and he mentioned that you had been to see him. Let me speak to them and see if we can expedite that. Routinely, though, I would get another opinion from an independent medical examiner, just so that we are not caught on the back foot in court. I will try to get that done in the next few days.'

'Thanks, Rudo.' Diara hesitated, then said, 'What will happen to Mum? Will she get bail?'

'It's unusual to get bail in murder cases. Even if the judge agrees, he will set a huge surety. Plus, your mum will have to hand in her passport and report daily, or even twice daily, to the police station. The police won't even consider bail until they have completed their investigations.'

Rudo looked down at her file and leafed through the papers until she found what she needed. 'When Leanne telephoned me about your mum, I took the liberty of meeting the investigating officer. I gather from him that your mum gave the police a verbal statement when they arrived at the house. What she said resulted in her arrest. She then repeated her statement at the police station, and signed a written statement confessing to the crime. Apparently, the police offered to call her lawyer, but she refused and said she did not know any lawyers.'

'But she did not mean to kill him,' said Diara. 'He was beating her, and she wanted him to stop.'

'Yes, that's essentially what her statement says – she was sleeping, and he came home drunk and wanted her to rub his back. She was not feeling well and had taken some pain meds. Apparently, when she did not comply, he started beating her. She said she got out of bed to escape from him, but he blocked the door. At this stage he was beating her with his fists, so she ran back towards the bed. He followed her and took off his belt and managed to get it round her throat. He was using the belt to strangle her. She says that she managed to kick him in the groin, then he released her and vomited. That was when she picked up the lamp and hit him on the head.' Rudo had been reading from a copy of Sophia Kruger's statement, which the police had provided. She looked at Diara, who was looking out of the window. She waited a few minutes for Diara to speak, then, when nothing was forthcoming, she continued. 'Is that what your mum told you?'

'More or less.'

'Okay. So, it will take a few weeks for the report from the medical examiner to come in. In the meantime, I have already arranged for photographs to be taken of your mum's injuries – which were extensive – and she has been examined by the government medical officer. This should help with our defence.'

'What can we do to help?'

'Diara, the police said that they responded to a domestic violence call from your Ambuya.'

'Yes.'

'Did that happen often?'

'Do you mean, did my father drink and hit Mum? Yep. For my whole life.'

'Do you know if your mum ever reported him to the police?'

'Not as far as I know. But she may have in the beginning. My recollection is that Mum just sucked it up and the day after, she acted like nothing had happened.'

'I will have to check with the Mabelreign Police Station if they have any reports of other incidents. This may take a while, because they are in the early stages of computerising, so it will mean looking through files of incident reports. I think it would help if you and your elder sister made statements about your father's violence.'

'I can do that. I'm not sure if Shaan is strong enough, though. She is still inconsolable. I think going to court will be difficult for her.'

'Look, it's early days and the wounds are fresh. But we need Shaan's testimony, because it will corroborate your mum's statement. There is a possibility that the prosecution may accept your mum's statement as the facts – then there would be no need for Shaan to testify. If the facts of the incident are not in dispute, then it means that the prosecution will only question her intention. Did she plan to kill him, or was it self-defence?'

Diara remained silent and continued to stare out of the window.

'Let's not decide anything right now. It will take well over a year for the matter to be heard.'

'A year!' Diara exclaimed. 'That's a long time.'

'Yes, unfortunately there's an enormous backlog of cases. Is there anyone else who may be able to give evidence of the ongoing domestic violence?'

'Well, there's our Ambuya. She has been with us since I was little. I'm not sure whether she will be willing, but you could ask her.'

'Anyone else? Did your mum have any close friends or family she might have confided in?'

'We have no other family here, and Mum didn't really have any friends. My father didn't like her to have any.'

'In that case, perhaps we can get an evaluation of your mum done by a psychologist or psychiatrist. I think it could be useful. Also, don't worry about giving evidence in open court. The law has recently been amended to allow evidence to be given in a separate room if the witness is considered vulnerable, or if the nature of the evidence is sensitive. This is supposed to lessen the trauma of speaking in open court in front of everyone. I am sure that Shaan will be able to manage in such circumstances.'

Diara took a deep breath, then started a conversation in an area she did not like to revisit. 'Um, there is someone else I was in touch with when I was at school. She was a psychologist at Parirenatywa Hospital.'

'Do you remember her name?'

'It was Mandy … Mandy Kaputa. I'm not sure if she's still there.'

Rudo made a note in her file. 'Okay. I'll contact her, see what she has to say. I'm going to wait for all the evidence to come in before I decide on the focus of my defence. But there are some issues to consider. It will be difficult for the prosecution to prove that your mum planned and plotted to kill your dad. She was sleeping, he woke her, he beat her, *and* he tried to strangle her. In fact, her life was threatened. Legally, this lesser charge is called self-defence. This is what I will probably set my sights on proving. If we can prove that she was protecting herself from imminent danger or threat of danger, this is legally considered a full defence and she will be found not guilty.

'However, if neither we nor the prosecution can prove our case, the judge may find her guilty of culpable homicide. This means that, although your father's death may have been an accident, your mum failed to avoid actions that resulted in his death. She picked up a heavy carved malachite lamp and hit him on the head. There is an assumption that if you hit someone on the head with a heavy object, you are aware that this may result in death.'

'What's the maximum sentence for culpable homicide?'

'Life.' Rudo hesitated, then added, 'But it does take the death penalty off the table.'

'Oh God, there really is no justice in the world, is there?'

'No, my dear. Not for women and children – as you well know from your own work. But please don't think the worst. The last time someone was sentenced to death in Zimbabwe was in 2005. The rules of evidence with respect to that are very clear, and this case comes nowhere near the scenario of irrefutable evidence that this murder was planned. In other words, how can the prosecution prove that this was planned? Having said that, Diara, I want you to be clear about the obstacles we face, so that we can come up with the best possible defence together.'

'I want that too.'

'Right. I'm going to remind you of a few facts. Almost two-thirds of the murder cases that go through the courts in Zimbabwe are domestic violence cases. The average sentence for men who kill their partners here – and, in fact, around the world – is two to six years. In the UK, according to government statistics, 46 per cent of murdered women are killed by a partner or ex-partner. You don't need me to remind you that O.J. Simpson was acquitted of killing his ex-wife and her friend after a trial that lasted eight months. But when a woman dares to kill her husband or partner, her average sentence is around fifteen years – even if she can prove that he had repeatedly beaten her over a long period, and even if she is able to show she acted in self-defence.'

The room was silent as Rudo allowed Diara to absorb her words. After a few minutes, Diara looked at Rudo.

'I know all that, Rudo. I have always known. The lives of women and children are cheap and expendable.'

'They certainly are,' Rudo responded sympathetically. 'But we're not giving up – we just need to understand the obstacles we face so that we can best prepare our defence. Right?'

Diara gave Rudo a grateful smile.

'Let's work towards finding facts that will mitigate the sentence. We need to find out why your mum behaved in such a violent manner. Look, it's not all doom and gloom. Domestic violence legislation now exists in Zimbabwe, and awareness is increasing. But we need to be realistic: we have a handicap even before we begin. The sentences I mention indicate that the judge's sympathies are usually with the man, no matter how flawed he is.'

4

LONDON, 2007

Diara returned to London, where she was snowed under with work. Everywhere she looked, she was presented with deadlines. Then she had numerous calls from Shaan – mostly about the trauma she had witnessed, sometimes asking for help. As a result, Diara had seen little of Leanne.

Rudo had also emailed her to give her a summary of the pathologist's report. There were no surprises there. The report had concluded that André Kruger had died from a blow to the back of the head with a heavy object. He had got off lightly in death, considering how much pain he had inflicted on his family during his lifetime, Diara thought. One blow to the head and too drunk to notice. Some people have all the luck.

Rudo had not managed to secure bail for Sophia but was hoping to apply again soon. The thought of her mother being incarcerated caused Diara enormous pain. She found that it continually infiltrated her thoughts. So much was going on in her head that she found it difficult to concentrate on anything else. Conversations were difficult, too. Often, her mind would wander off to other, more pressing issues. However, she had mastered the art of smiling and nodding appropriately. Given her state of mind, she found it easier to spend most of her evenings and spare time on her own. Her restlessness, and her guilt that her sisters were having to cope on their own, consumed her life.

Leanne tried hard to arrange outings for them, but she failed. She took to going over to Diara's flat and sitting there with her. When she rang Diara and invited her to come over for dinner the next day, she knew that she had to ask in a way that would make it difficult for Diara to refuse. Luckily, when she rang, she got her voicemail.

'Hi, Diara, hope you're good. Could I ask an enormous favour, please? Please come over for dinner tomorrow night. Xander is here visiting. I have a long day at school tomorrow. Please come over – I really need help. Also, could you bring a dessert? Sorry to be such a pain. Thank you so, so much. Love you. See you tomorrow. Usual time.'

❁❁❁

The next evening, Diara made her way to Leanne and Aidan's home. It was a bitterly cold December night, and the light rain felt icy against her face. She was carrying a supermarket carrier bag containing the ingredients to make an Eton mess: cream, meringues, fresh strawberries. She had not checked her voicemail until this morning, and it was the only dessert she could think of that could be made at the last minute and that did not require skill or intelligence.

Leanne opened the door and hugged her enthusiastically. 'Hello, dearest! Come in.'

Diara followed her into the hallway and took off her coat. The hallway led straight to the lounge, and Diara could see Aidan and Xander in there, laughing over their drinks. They stood up in response to Leanne's cheery call that Diara was here.

'Hello, Diara.' Aidan greeted her with a tight hug and a gentle kiss on her hair. Diara hugged him back and kissed him on the cheek. He rubbed his cheek. 'Those are really cold lips, my darling!'

Diara smiled and turned to the other guest, in whose honour she had been dragged here. She smiled at Xander Joubert and hugged him briefly and awkwardly. Xander had to lean down to hug her – she was at least six inches shorter than he was. He was tall, with a strong frame. His sandy brown hair had been bleached by the sun and his skin was tanned a nut brown. His face was saved from being considered ordinary by his dark turquoise eyes and his crooked ready smile.

He stepped back and smiled at her. 'You look well.'

Alexander Joubert had been in Diara's friendship group at university. He had been Leanne's friend to begin with, and that was how Diara had met him. From the moment they met, she had been attracted to him and he had become the secret object of her fascination. This attraction came as a surprise to both girls. Diara had not shown interest in any boys until then. She had refused to go to the school O level dance for this reason. Leanne had declared that she would not go to the dance without Diara. In the end, they had gone to the dance without partners and had spent the evening dancing together. This became the norm for them when attending parties. They were happy to dance with each other or alone.

But Xander was different. There were so many things she loved about him. He spoke softly and his smile was never far away. He had a way of letting her know that she was part of the conversation, even though she hardly spoke when the group met up between lectures at the Students' Union. Xander had a way of teasing her that eroded her defences. She and Leanne spent many an hour discussing

41

her secret feelings for him. However, her feelings remained a secret. Xander had gone on to marry Saskia, a suitable girl from a wealthy South African family.

Saskia's family had emigrated from England to South Africa in the mid-1800s. She failed to mention that these ancestors of hers arrived to work in the gold mines, where they exploited the local people by employing them to risk their lives in dangerous mines to harvest gold. However, Saskia boasted that her ancestors had been close to Cecil John Rhodes and had worked with him in one of the big finance houses.

'Well, that's not something I would boast about, Saskia. It's not like Rhodes had a good reputation,' Leanne had told her.

Diara and Leanne were mixed race. They had been brought up in an environment of racial discrimination and injustice and were suspicious of Saskia. This was not surprising, given the circumstances in which they had been raised. Colonial Zimbabwe was as racially divided as South Africa with its apartheid laws, but in Zimbabwe this was called the colour bar policy. This divided society into black and white. Cecil John Rhodes had set the precedent for this attitude in the 1890s. Rhodes had believed that it was the job of the British to civilise the Africans. Thus began a process whereby the white settlers 'civilised' Africans by treating them as children requiring guidance. After all, there were so many of them, they should be controlled. And control them they did. This control stretched to the use of violence.

Growing up, both girls had experienced the effects of the policy in their daily lives. Legally, people of an Asian or 'coloured' background could only live in certain designated areas. 'Coloureds' in colonial Zimbabwe were people of mixed race claiming both European and African descent. Some suburbs were categorised as 'African' areas – but the best areas were, of course, for the use of white people. The only Africans who could live in these areas were employed as 'houseboys' or 'garden boys'. They usually lived at the bottom of the garden, beyond the swimming pool and tennis court, in basic cottages called *kayas*. They were expected to shop for their employers, but they were rarely allowed to enter shops. White shoppers were 'disturbed' by them. Instead, they were served through the 'big black hole'. Leanne had coined this phrase for the hatch on the side walls of shops through which non-white people were served.

Diara had always been interested in the effects of violence in apartheid South Africa and colonial Zimbabwe. Apartheid may have been similar to the colour bar, as written policies go. However, there were huge differences in the way these policies were rolled out. It was easier to control Zimbabwe's population of ten million than the sixty million in South Africa, so in South Africa rules were harsher and levels of violence greater. Obviously, these settlers had more to lose. The resources in South Africa were unparalleled in the rest of Africa. As a result, South Africa suffered a longer history of colonisation than Zimbabwe. The white minority was not willing to give up a country so rich in gold, diamonds, platinum, iron ore and numerous other minerals, and the high levels of violence used to maintain control resulted in dehumanising people and led to unmanageable levels of crimes such as carjacking. At least carjacking and 'necklacing' were unheard of in Zimbabwe. 'Necklacing' was the practice of forcing a tyre filled with petrol around the neck of someone suspected of colluding with the police, then setting it alight. It was usual for victims of carjacking to be pumped full of bullets, the shooter apparently feeling little or no remorse.

Although state-sponsored racism in Zimbabwe ended with the advent of independence in 1980 and the end of white minority rule, entrenched attitudes were harder to erase. Independence brought with it policies of reconciliation. Robert Mugabe, Zimbabwe's first black prime minister, said at the Independence Day celebrations, 'The wrongs of the past must stand forgiven and forgotten'. Very poetic – but the race issues had been years in the making, and would require the same amount of time to be undone.

Diara recalled a time during their first year at varsity when the group had gone to a birthday party at a home in the northern suburbs. The northern suburbs were formerly where the elite whites resided. Leanne had been invited by a French girl whose father worked in the French Embassy. They had met in their French literature class. Marianne had extended the invitation to the whole group, who she had met a few times in the Students' Union.

The party was held outdoors, with a live band and a buffet dinner. Leanne had pulled Diara onto the dance floor, where the band played a very credible version of 'Jabulani'. The song – meaning 'rejoice' – was usually sung by a South African artist. It was one of the girls' favourite dance numbers, with its catchy beat. They were soon joined by Xander and Cecil. The latter, was another of their varsity friends. Cecil, of course, was dancing with his beer bottle – normal behaviour for him. Unfortunately, that night his overenthusiastic dancing resulted in his beer bottle flying off and hitting the arm of a white man talking to his girlfriend at the edge of the dance floor.

The white couple were incensed, and the man immediately strode over to Cecil. Xander had intervened when Cecil's apology fell on deaf ears. The white man was prodding Cecil in the chest and snarling.

'Hey man, we are really sorry. I hope that you're not hurt.'

'Who the fuck are you? Stay out of it!'

Cecil had stopped apologising and was becoming belligerent. Leanne and Diara, seeing the danger, began to drag him away. Other people were looking over, showing an interest in the argument. Xander, who generally avoided conflict, turned to follow them but stopped when the aggrieved man said, 'Off you go, bloody pussy! Don't let us keep you. I hear that these kaffir bitches are good at blow jobs.' He and his girlfriend tittered, and she covered her mouth in a gesture of modesty. The next minute, both boys were on him. Xander held him tightly, pinning his arms, while Cecil held him by the throat and said quietly but with menace, 'Look, man, I really can't answer your question. But I'm thinking, maybe your girl can give us a demonstration so that we can compare them ...'

The man tried to backtrack. 'Leave her out of it. She didn't do anything to you.'

'Neither did our friends. They were just minding their own business.'

At this stage, others had intervened to pull them apart, and Leanne managed to drag Cecil towards the car park. Xander and Diara followed. Leanne pushed Cecil into the back of her mum's car and used a tissue and water from her water bottle to wipe his lip, which was bleeding. Diara took the keys from Leanne and moved towards the driver's seat.

'Are you all right to drive, Dee? Let me drive – I've only had half a beer,' Xander said. He put his arm around Diara and led her to the passenger side. She was in tears.

'I'm all right. It just reminded me of the sly looks and sniggers I used to get from white boys in the Students' Union. And all the times we were called names when I was growing up.' She wiped her eyes.

45

In the car, everyone was quiet, lost in thought. After a few minutes, the northern suburbs were in the distance. Xander spoke again without taking his eyes off the road. 'I'm sorry, guys. That was so rude.'

'Why are you apologising? You didn't say anything rude!' Leanne was quick to snap back. Then Xander stopped to drop Cecil off outside his gate. The atmosphere was uncomfortable, and Diara knew that they were all having similar thoughts: that the stereotype of black women representing everything carnal to white men lived on. White men believed that black women had lascivious, uncontrolled sexuality in comparison to white women, who were portrayed as modest, pure and respectful.

It had been a shock to the girls when Xander married Saskia a couple of years later. She was a perfect example of someone who considered herself racially superior, but her condescending attitude was a front for her fear of all non-white persons. Saskia's family, purely by virtue of their colour, enjoyed free schooling, health care and business opportunities. The friends had met Xander's wife a few times, they tolerated her – for Xander's sake. They were not unkind to her, but they didn't attempt to bond with her or try to get to know her better. To give Saskia credit, she picked up their cues and stopped sharing personal information with them. Their conversation was usually superficial and pleasant. Diara's conversations with her rarely went beyond an initial greeting.

❁❁❁

'Where's Saskia?' Diara asked, looking around. She had assumed that Xander would be with his wife.

'This is a boys' trip. Anyway, she's been staying with her parents in Cape Town for a while.'

'Is she feeling any better?'

Saskia had suffered two miscarriages, and this had resulted in clinical depression. Diara had heard from Leanne that after her second miscarriage, Saskia had not emerged from her room for over two weeks. Her behaviour had oscillated between hysterical weeping and stony silences. She would not communicate with Xander at all, and he was finally forced to ask her parents to step in.

'Much better. She's ready to come home next weekend.'

Diara made all the right noises, then thankfully was saved from any further conversation about Saskia when Leanne called them in to dinner. Dinner turned out to be pleasant, with Xander talking mostly about his ski trip in the Alps. It was only towards the end of the meal that Aidan mentioned in passing that Diara had been away at her father's funeral. Xander was suitably sympathetic and asked appropriate questions, which she answered without giving away too much detail.

'Had my father been ill? No.'

Leanne saved Diara from any further questions by bringing in coffee and tea. Soon after coffee, Diara got up to leave. She felt too tired to sit and talk any more, even though she was with her closest friends.

'I'd better go too. My plane is at nine tomorrow morning.' Xander got up to leave, joining Diara in the entrance hall as she was putting on her coat.

'Let me walk you to your flat, Diara. It's on the way to the Tube.'

Although the temperature was in the low single figures, it had stopped raining, so the walk was pleasant. Xander went back to the topic of her father's death, and Diara realised she had to give him more details. 'Look, Xander, the thing is … my mum said that she killed him.'

'What? What do you mean? Literally or figuratively?'

'Literally.'

Shock and compassion were apparent on his face. 'What the hell? Are you having me on?' But he could see that she was serious. They had reached Diara's flat. She wanted to avoid any further discussion, so she began to hunt through her bag for her keys. She located them and turned to say goodbye to him. He was standing staring at her and running his hands through his hair.

'Well, it was good to see you, Xander. Give my best to Saskia.'

'Diara, you can't just chuck that at me then leave!' He stared at her, aghast. She kept quiet and looked away. She didn't want to say anything. It was too hard to keep her tears in check. Xander took the keys from her hand, opened the door and indicated for her to precede him. 'Can I come in for a bit?' he asked after following her up the short flight of stairs to her apartment. He did not wait for her response, but closed and locked the door behind him. 'What happened?' he asked gently, taking her hand and walking her over to the sofa in the lounge.

'Well, Mum's not saying much. The police said that they responded to a domestic violence call-out from Ambuya. They arrived and found the house in disarray and my father dead on the bedroom floor.'

'Did they say how? Did your mum say?'

Diara told him briefly what had transpired, inwardly cringing. *God,* she thought, *why couldn't I have had regular parents?*

'Bloody hell, Diara! How are you?'

Diara shrugged. 'It's all a bit much to take in. Also, I feel terrible having to come back to London and leave Shaan and Ambuya to look after the two girls, run the house and so on. I can't ask for a transfer back to

Zimbabwe now, not after I worked so hard to get the move to the London office. I need my job, because we need the money to survive. It's such a mess, Xander.'

She felt him squeeze her hand in sympathy.

'Are you okay, Dee?'

Initially, Diara was confused by the question. 'I'm fine. Just worried about Mum. The police are charging her with murder, but her lawyer is preparing a self-defence case, in the hope that Mum will be found not guilty.'

'I guess she won't be granted bail?'

'No. Apparently not.'

They were lost in their own thoughts for a while.

Xander broke the silence. Hesitantly he asked, 'So … the violence … did it happen often?' He added quickly, 'I know this must be very painful. Please don't answer if you don't want to. I shouldn't pry. Sorry.'

'It's fine. I don't mind talking about it now. You're one of very few people I have discussed it with. And to answer your question, yep. It happened as far back as I can remember. There was always something to set him off.' Diara's eyes became unfocused as she stared past Xander and out of the window. 'We were all scared of him. When we were little, we blamed the beer. It was only when I was older that I realised that the alcohol was just a facilitator. It helped him to be exactly what he was – a violent, disrespectful thug.'

'Did you ever try telling anyone or asking for help?'

'Once or twice. But nothing really came of it. And no matter how hard I try, I can't forgive Mum for not standing up to him. She never did anything to protect us. I know that she was a victim too, that he beat any courage out of her, but I can't help thinking that if those were my children, I would have done anything to get them away from him.'

'Diara, we can't judge her. We did not live her life.'

'I know. I know all that. But I can't forgive her.'

'I'm sure you will, with time.'

'You think? When I was little, I was so terrified when he was around that the only way I could cope with it was to go away to happy places in my mind. They were usually where one of the other kids in the class had been. A holiday. A Princess Jasmine birthday party. A visit to Water World, where I was sliding down the longest slide, screaming with joy.' Diara spoke in an expressionless voice.

Xander sat in silence, still squeezing her hand.

Diara glanced at him. The compassion she saw on his face made her want to weep. She tried to smile, although some tears had squeezed out. 'Anyway, that's all in the past. He's dead and it's time to move on.'

'Was this going on at varsity?'

'Yes. Although I was saved from it, largely, because I lived on campus. I spent most of my holidays with Leanne. She and her family literally saved my life.' Suddenly, she just wanted to be alone. A great melancholy had enveloped her. She stood up. She wanted him to go away so she could be on her own and not have to rehash the story. She did that enough on her own. Diara knew she was being dismissive and rude, but she didn't care. 'Please don't let me keep you – you have an early flight.' She moved forward to embrace him, as was customary. He returned the embrace and, as she moved away, he held on to her hand.

'Dee, wait. If you need anything, anything at all, just ask. Okay?'

She nodded and moved away, as she could feel her control slipping again. 'Well, see you soon,' she said awkwardly, standing by the door. He sighed and got up to go.

'Okay, I'll go. I just thought maybe it would help to talk

more about it. I meant what I said – if there is anything I can do to help, just ask.' He had his hands on her shoulders as he emphasised his last point, then he leant down to kiss her on her cheek. Perhaps more to comfort himself than her – a normal human response. But Diara felt her outward control crumble and held on to him, finally looking for comfort.

They held each other for a while. Xander stroked her hair and made soothing, appropriate noises. His stroking was hesitant and awkward, and she sensed his helplessness. She felt a rush of tenderness for him. She knew she was feeling too much for him. She stretched up to kiss his cheek, but somehow it was not his cheek she found. They were both willing participants initially, but when the temperature and intensity of the kiss changed, Diara's common sense came to the fore. She pushed him away, angry at all the events of the past month and her embarrassment at losing control, so angry that she lifted her right hand and slapped him.

Xander jerked back in shock. 'Diara …'

'Just shut up, Xander. Don't say anything.' She rubbed her face, breathing heavily. 'Why did you do that?' she asked him accusingly. 'I wasn't good enough for you at varsity, was I? Too much colour for your taste, not white enough – so what's changed?'

Diara knew she was sounding like a shrew, but she couldn't stop herself. The person she had always thought of so highly had become a target for her anger. Somewhere in the back of her mind she knew that she was being unreasonable and probably sounding ridiculous, but that didn't stop her. 'What's wrong? Did your perfect white wife not live up to your expectations? And suddenly I am good enough!'

'What the fuck, Diara? Stop it. You sound crazy. Do

51

you remember what happened the last time I tried to ask you out?'

His comment incensed her even more. She gave an incredulous, humourless laugh. 'Asked me out? Is that the new synonym for groping me when you were plastered? I remember that differently.' Roughly, she prodded her temple with a finger.

'Do you know how difficult it was to be around you? You were hardly the most approachable person. But could you not see how I felt?' he asked.

'You mean, how you felt about me when your filter was off?'

Xander was quiet. Diara was exhausted and drained. 'Go home, Xander. Go back to your wife.'

5

XANDER JOUBERT

Xander left Diara's apartment and made his way to the Tube station. He walked briskly so that he could block out what had just happened. Only once he was at the station, on the platform waiting for the train, did he think about it. He felt like a fool. He stamped his foot in frustration. What had come over him? Had seeing her rekindled old feelings? Or was it something else?

Xander closed his eyes. Immediately, the the apple-scent of her hair drifted back to him. The near imperceptible movement of her lips under his. That beautiful, generous mouth. Her hands stretching out to touch his hair gently. Soft, soft murmurs of pleasure. He almost groaned aloud as he remembered the feel of her pressed against him. Such a far cry from the quiet, private girl he remembered from varsity. All he had known about her was that she smiled at him occasionally and sometimes he caught her watching him.

His dating behaviour at varsity had not helped him to get closer to her. He had noticed her faint air of disapproval when they discussed his dates, break-ups and one-night stands. She never seemed to have any. There was no way he could ask her out when she knew all about his intimate relationships. He groaned and hit his forehead with the heel of his hand. He opened his eyes, suddenly realising where he was, and grateful that the other passengers didn't seem to have noticed his behaviour.

He was ashamed to admit that she was right about the race issues. They had grown up in a society where segregation was encouraged by the government and the community. Segregation existed in schools, public toilets, restaurants and even some shops. Although its extent and enforcement in the then Rhodesia was not at the level normally associated with apartheid in South Africa, it had still been a way of life for them. He would be lying to himself if he denied that her race had been one factor that had stopped him asking her out. When he told his male friends about his attraction to her, they were not supportive.

'Don't go up that road,' his friend Cecil had advised, 'unless you feel really strongly about her. It's not an easy road to travel.'

Xander had reluctantly agreed to give himself time – time to decide if his attraction to her was transitory or longer-lasting. His friend had a point. He could imagine the horror and disbelief on his parents' faces if he took Diara home for dinner. Perhaps they would not show their feelings in her presence, but afterwards he would have to listen to lectures about the pitfalls of 'such relationships'. Diara was probably in a similar position. However, he found that time did not help. In fact, it made it more difficult for him to approach her. His attraction to her remained. She intrigued him. Diara maintained a cool distance from all except a chosen few. She underplayed her assets by choosing to wear gender-neutral clothes – jeans, T-shirts or button-down shirts, whatever the occasion, along with her customary black eyeliner. But this did not detract from her exotic face or stop him lusting after her.

Eventually, an incident on a group night out had made him realise that perhaps his attraction was one-sided. They had gone out to celebrate his birthday. They usually all went out together in one car, which belonged to Leanne's mother. Diara was the designated driver as she did not drink. That night, beer and wine had been flowing, and all were merrier than usual. He was the last one to be dropped off before the girls went home. Leanne was asleep in the front, and he was dozing in the back, reluctant to move. Diara drove up the long, narrow driveway to his house and waited for him to get out. To be fair, he had tried to open the door but for some reason, it hadn't budged. Finally, Diara had flounced out of the car with a long-suffering sigh and opened the door for him. She grabbed his arm and helped him out.

'Come on, Xander, let's get you inside.'

He remembered leaning heavily on her; he was unsteady on his feet. She was almost bent over sideways under his weight. At the front door, he dug around in his pockets for his key, but it kept evading his fingers.

'Where is your key? Have you lost it?'

He'd mumbled some response and carried on trying to dig the key out of his jeans pocket. Diara let go of his arm, pushed his arm away, put her hand into his pocket and pulled the key out. She opened the front door and gave him a little push towards it. 'Go on, get inside. I can't wait here all night.'

He knew she was annoyed, but he just stared at her blankly until she shook him and reminded him again to go in. He mumbled his thanks and leant down to hug her, but unfortunately the hug became amorous very quickly. The only way he could describe it, thinking back, was that he had slobbered all over her face while holding her tight against him. She was trying to get away, pushing him hard and repeatedly telling him to stop. He responded by telling her all about his long-term attraction to her and her physical attributes.

Eventually she managed to push him off her. He stumbled and fell. She looked at him in disgust and walked off without a backward glance. Even now, thinking of the incident was mortifying. Not his finest moment. After that, relations had been strained between them for a few weeks, even though he had apologised on Monday. She had glared at him and told him never to do it again. That was when Xander had concluded that perhaps Diara was not attracted to him. It took a long time for her to feel relaxed in his company again; the damage had been done. Things were never the same after that. She was even more reserved with him than with the others.

He had moved to South Africa after graduating, and had sent everyone in the group his phone number and address. She had thanked him, but never got in touch. She had also been noticeably absent on his wedding day, having sent a stilted message wishing him well. She had been the only one from their group who had not attended. Over the years, he had seen Diara occasionally, usually at events arranged by Leanne, never initiated by Diara.

He sighed and rubbed his hands over his face, trying to wipe out his most recent memory. He had done it again, and this time he couldn't even blame alcohol.

6
JOHANNESBURG, 2008

Diara grabbed her bag off carousel number two in the baggage claim hall at O.R. Tambo International Airport in Johannesburg and started to walk quickly towards the exit. Ten days ago, she had arrived in Zimbabwe to attend a Child First meeting of all project managers in the region. She was there to represent head office in London. Now she was on her way back to London, and she was making a brief stop in Jo'burg for the night. Her connecting flight was early the next morning – which would give her the opportunity to right a wrong.

She had taken the opportunity to buy enough food for her family for the next few months, such as rice, flour and other dry goods. The freezer was full of meat. This meant that Shaan or Ambuya would only have to buy perishables. Her mum, sadly, had not changed her mind about her testimony. Diara had given up trying to persuade her otherwise. Rudo had decided they would have to find an alternative way to tell the court about all that Sophia had suffered at her husband's hands, since she refused to make a statement in her own defence. She still insisted on blaming herself for her husband's violence.

Now that Diara was on her way back to London, she felt a sense of relief. As she rushed through the arrivals hall, the sticky afternoon heat wrapped itself around her. Beads of sweat gathered on her face and she felt a trickle of sweat run down her back. She stopped for a minute to get her bearings, then headed for the exit.

Outside, she crossed the road and hurried towards the airport hotel she had booked online last night. All around her, vehicles were arriving to collect passengers, amid numerous construction vehicles. Building work was ongoing at the airport in preparation for the football World Cup, which would be hosted by South Africa in 2010. The dust and noise of the construction work overpowered her senses.

With a sigh of relief, Diara stepped into the air-conditioned hotel. It was a familiar and comforting sight. Diara often stayed there when she worked in Zimbabwe. It was a convenient place to break a journey before catching or returning from long-haul flights. She had routed her flight back to London through Johannesburg. Her employer preferred their employees to use British airline – unless of course there was an emergency, when the fastest route was recommended.

'Diara Kruger. I have a reservation.'

The well-trained, smiling receptionist glanced at her computer screen. 'Yes, Ms Kruger, your room is ready. Would you kindly complete this form? I will need to take a copy of your passport.'

As Diara completed the registration form, she glanced at the clock behind the reception desk. Five o'clock. Only an hour before she had to be ready. She felt anxious and agitated at once. She gave the completed form and her passport to the receptionist and breathed in deeply, trying to infuse her mind with serenity.

She made her way to her room on the fourth floor. Once there, she hastily unpacked her toiletries and a change of clothing. She took out a simple white cotton shift dress which left her arms and legs below the knee bare. After a quick shower, she dressed and redid her make-up. She did the best she could with the little she had. As she lined her eyes with black eyeliner, she was assailed by doubts again – doubts about the way she looked, who she was, and the enormous one: that she was not going to cope with the task at hand.

Her heart was beating fast and her chest felt tight. *Don't be ridiculous, Diara. Pull yourself together.* It wasn't working. She was flapping her hands around, trying to stop herself wheezing. Overwhelmed, she sat down abruptly on the closed toilet seat, breathing deeply. Slowly, she took herself to a place of comfort: lying on the couch at Leanne's house, talking, and listening to Cat Stevens. As she began to feel calmer, she reached for her hairbrush on the vanity and brushed her almost waist-length hair. The deep, steady strokes were the ultimate comfort. When she had finished, she picked up her handbag and room key and made her way to the lift. As soon as she entered the restaurant on the ground floor, she saw him. He was sitting at the bar, holding a drink and chatting to the bartender, who was placing a small plate of fancy nuts in front of him.

God, she thought, *this is it*. Again she felt her courage faltering.

She took a step. Mentally, she admonished herself for being ridiculous and cowardly. She moved forward then hesitated again. *Can I do this? Yes, I can. Of course I can! It's just a date. No, silly, it's not a date. Meeting a friend for dinner? Yes. Yes. Go, Diara. Leave it to the gods.*

She walked towards him with determination. Her father's death had changed her, made her more confident.

'Hey, Xander.'

When he heard his name, Xander stood up immediately and smiled.

There was no awkward hug today. Too much had happened between them. She realised that she had to say something to him, so they could try to put the London incident behind them. Although she had emailed him a few days afterwards to apologise and he had responded favourably, she knew they had unfinished business, despite the five months that had passed since they had met in London.

'Thanks for coming out here to meet me. I could have met you nearer your home or office.'

'It's fine, honestly. I could do with the break. Saskia is in Cape Town this week and I have been flat out working on a presentation for a new client we're hoping to land.'

Xander was a project manager for a large advertising company in South Africa.

'How is Saskia?' Diara asked once they were seated at their table. 'Pity she is away; she could have joined us.'

Xander looked up in surprise from studying the menu, then laughed.

Diara stared at him. He had a contagious laugh, which involved his whole face. The blue of his irises appeared bluer, laughter lines crinkled around his eyes, and the dimple in his chin looked more pronounced. He ran his hand through his thick hair, which was always untidy and wild. It was a little curly and had a mind of its own.

'For some reason, Sas has the impression that you don't like her.'

Diara went still, taken aback by this. It was true, but it wasn't personal. Childishly, she had never liked any of his girlfriends. She thought it best not to comment.

'I guess she's just not used to you. Like we are,' he added hastily.

'So how is she doing?'

'Well, better than she was when I saw you in London. She still has down times, but now she has more good days.'

Conveniently, the waiter arrived with water and bread rolls for the table. Diara grabbed a menu and studied it with total concentration. Anything to stop the discussion about Xander's wife – she felt angry with herself for starting it.

'What are you having, Xander? My treat.'

Xander studied the menu while Diara studied him. 'I'm starving. I feel like I haven't eaten for days. I've been working overtime on this bid. Two nights ago, I fell asleep at my desk and the cleaner found me at five in the morning.' They laughed. 'I hope you won't regret that offer.' He looked up and smiled at her. Diara smiled back.

'Order whatever you want. You can always offer to have sex with the manager after!'

They looked at the overweight, bald, fifty-something manager, who had a harassed look on his face.

'The venison carpaccio sounds interesting, and I think I'll have the bouillabaisse to follow.'

'Bouillabaisse? What's that?' Diara scanned the menu, looking for an explanation. It was described as fish broth infused with saffron. 'Looks good, but I think I'll have the chickpea and biltong salad and the gem squash risotto. Two things I miss in London – biltong and gem squash. They are there if you know where to look, but they're outlandishly priced.'

'Are they the only two things you miss? How about your family? You must miss them.'

'I miss my mum and sisters.'

'And Zim? Do you miss the sunshine?'

'I did at first. But then the weather in London got less important. I love my life in London. I feel safe there. Besides, Leanne is there, and that's wonderful.'

The conversation stopped for a while as the waiter cleared the empty starter plates. Diara decided that this was as good a time as any to say what she had to. 'Xander, I wanted to apologise to you about what happened when we last met in London. I was overwrought and devastated about what had happened with Mum, and I took it out on you. It was wrong and I said some very cruel things. Worse, I should never have slapped you. Please forgive me.' Diara felt tearful just thinking of the things she had said to him. A tear rolled down her cheek, and she wiped it away angrily. Xander held up his hand to stop her, then ran his fingers through his hair.

'No, Diara, you don't get to do that. You don't get to make me feel better. I was wrong. You were right. I have a wife, and had no business touching you like I did. I just felt so bad that you were hurting and there was nothing I could do to help. But I was wrong to take advantage of you at your most vulnerable.' He leant over and took her hand and squeezed it. 'I would really appreciate it if you didn't cry. I'm useless in situations where crying is involved. I just want us to go back to the friendship we had, please. Okay?'

She nodded.

'You sure you don't want any wine?'

'No, water is good. I have a long flight tomorrow, so it's best to keep hydrated. Also, you know I don't drink.'

'Just teasing. By the way, how much money did you earn from being the designated driver on our nights out?'

Diara recalled the rules that had applied on the group's nights out at varsity. She was always the designated driver. Leanne would pick everyone up and Diara would take everyone home, the two girls in the front and the four boys squashed into the back. If they were drunk, the fee was ten dollars for a safe trip home. However, if anyone was drunk and amorous, the fine doubled. Should anyone commit the cardinal sin of puking in the car, the fine went up to thirty dollars. Leanne was, of course, exempt from being charged.

'I have no idea, but it was a fair amount. Especially from Cecil. He could never pass up the opportunity to grope anything vaguely female. The worst thing was, as he was touching my bottom – or another part of my anatomy – he would add an insult.' Diara grimaced.

'What do you mean?'

'Well. You were probably too drunk to remember, but he would always say stuff like, "Diara, you have to do something about your butt, it's nonexistent! I need something I can grab hold of".'

'That sounds like him. Idiot!'

'Or he'd say, "Diara, have you heard of a Wonderbra? You really need to get one for those little mosquito bites you call boobs".'

Xander looked even more uncomfortable. Diara shrugged. 'That's Cecil for you. But he was the only one I ever charged the maximum fee. I figured I deserved it for putting up with his insults.'

'But you never let his behaviour when he was drunk get in the way of your relationship when he was sober. Why were you so unforgiving of me? Why did it take me ages to earn your forgiveness?'

Diara immediately grew defensive. She was angry that he had brought it up just when she thought they had reached an even keel. She looked away, tried to decide how to respond and decided that the truth was better. She did not want to sugar-coat it. 'I was angry with you. At least Cecil was honest in his groping. But you waited till you were drunk to tell me about your feelings. Why not tell me when you were sober? Did you even mean what you said? Or was it some sick game you boys had come up with? How was I to know whether you really meant it?'

'No one knows what happened that night except us. And yes, I meant what I said: I knew who you were and took the opportunity to kiss you.'

Diara was a little taken aback by his honesty. She had not expected it. She took a sip of water while he waited for her response, staring at her impassively. But she was not convinced. Since they were on the subject, she wanted all the questions that had dogged her for the past decade to be clarified. 'But if you meant it, why did you never ask me out at varsity? Was it because I was difficult – or repulsive?'

Now the conversation was getting too deep for Xander. His eyes met Diara's. Her expression was neutral, patiently waiting for a response. After what seemed like an eternity to Diara, he responded. 'I guess it was a combination of things. But you're not repulsive. Not at all.'

'What sort of things?'

'Well, first, I had no idea if you wanted me to tell you how I felt. I wanted to, but when I plucked up the courage to tell you, you told me never to touch you again. Second, I watched you reject any other man who tried to say more than hello to you.'

Diara continued looking at him, unblinking.

'Also, we were part of the same group – we all talked about our flings and relationships. We trashed each other. Trashed our dates. But you never did. You told us nothing about yourself. You just listened to our stories.'

'Okay, I can understand that. Did you think I was odd?'

'No ... no,' he said, seeming to be grappling for the right word. 'Just reserved.'

'What are you saying, Xander? That I was too weird for you?'

Xander sighed. 'You're killing me. No. It was complicated.'

Diara was not going to let him get off so easily. She asked him the delicate million-dollar question. 'Did it have anything to do with the fact that I was brown?'

Xander looked uncomfortable. He raked his hand through his hair, as if to calm himself. 'I'm ashamed to say that perhaps it did, to some extent. Cecil warned me that it wouldn't be easy starting a relationship with you. He didn't think my parents – or yours – would encourage it – he thought they would be against it. He advised me to give it some time and see whether I still felt strongly about you. But then I messed it up when I was drunk and you told me never to touch you again.'

Diara was silent in the face of his admission. Looking embarrassed, he turned away to look at the waiter approaching, carrying their mains. She was dazed by his honesty and unsure how to respond. Then she decided that he had been so honest that he deserved the same from her. 'Maybe it was the wrong place at the wrong time. I'm not sure. But when I met you, you wormed your way into my heart. No one has been able to replace you. I was just afraid of rejection or something, I'm not sure what.'

Xander was speechless. He realised this admission had been difficult for her and he leant over and took her hand again and squeezed it. She tried to smile in response but failed miserably. She squeezed his hand and then withdrew it as the waiter arrived with more wine.

'Sauvignon Blanc to complement your fish soup, sir,' he said, smiling.

'Really?' said Diara, rolling her eyes. 'They all smell the same to me.' She was glad of the opportunity to move on to a less emotional topic.

'Well, the theory is that venison is complemented by a red wine such as Shiraz or a Pinot Noir. But after a few glasses, it doesn't matter ...'

'If you say so. It's all Greek to me.'

Wine was the last thing on her mind. Her focus was on all the miscommunication between them. She largely blamed herself. She knew that she could be unapproachable. She had always tended to stay on the edge of their friendship group, friendly but reticent. She never went out with the boys without Leanne, for whatever reason.

Xander watched the emotions flash across her face. He didn't want her to crawl back into her shell or for them to go back to their former superficial friendship. He leant over and took her hand again. She was startled by the gesture. He waited for her to focus, gently rubbing her knuckles with his thumb. She eventually gave him a small smile.

'Look, Diara, I know I have hurt you and I'm truly sorry for that. I didn't behave well where you were concerned. I was immature and dishonest with myself. I didn't have the courage to be honest with you about how I felt. Let's move forward.'

Those seemed to be the magic words: her smile grew and she nodded in agreement. He pressed his lips to her knuckles. She squeezed his hand then quickly released it before lifting her glass to gulp some water.

'What else have you been up to? Outside of work? Anything interesting?'

'Well, Leanne and I went to a Lionel Richie concert. Does that count? And we saw Tracey Chapman at the Royal Albert Hall.'

'Those definitely count. I can't believe you still love Lionel.'

'Yep. Fan for life – and, before you ask, still obsessed with Cat Stevens.'

Conversation focused on the concerts and other activities that had occupied them since their last meeting. They laughed as Diara described a weekend when she and Leanne had binge-watched two seasons of *Sex and the City*. Diara felt herself relax. It was almost as if no one else and no other life existed at this moment. It was short-lived.

'Have you met anyone? Anyone interesting you want to spend time with? Have fun with?'

Diara was caught unawares by the question. She swallowed awkwardly and took a sip of water. 'Not yet. I'm still looking.'

'Looking for what, Diara? Are you really?' Xander looked sceptical.

'No,' she said after some consideration. 'I'm not. Not now. It's all been so hectic – moving to London and starting a new job. Also, I mostly work with women. And I haven't seen anyone on the Tube that I like the look of.'

'I guess it's difficult,' he said.

'And you know that I am not the easiest person to get on with.'

'So how are Leanne and Aidan?' he asked, switching subjects smoothly.

Diara started to share bits of information about Leanne and her husband. This she did on autopilot. But her mind was working overtime, analysing what he had said earlier.

When their mains were cleared, Diara realised that the restaurant was busy. All the tables were occupied, and alcohol-laced voices were escalating in volume. Most of the laughter was coming from a table of over twenty young men who looked like they belonged to a sports team.

'How does chocolate tart with peppermint crisp ice cream sound?' she asked.

'Magical.'

'Shall we have it sent with coffee to the lounge? It's really noisy here.'

'Good idea,' Xander agreed, and they made their way to the lounge near the bar outside the restaurant. There were very few people in the lounge, although the bar was crowded. They found a small table with two comfortable armchairs. As they sat down, the waiter arrived with their desserts and coffee.

✿✿✿

As the last piece of chocolate tart slipped down her throat, Diara shut her eyes and sighed, utterly content. 'Yum. That was beyond amazing.'

'You look like you enjoyed that.'

'You think?' She smiled. 'How about you?'

'Who wouldn't?'

'I'm gonna have to have a week of fennel tea to detox. Hey, did you know they don't sell peppermint crisp in London? Apparently it's local to South Africa. Leanne once found some at Selfridges and we were overjoyed. We would have a square every evening. It took us a week to eat the bar.'

They were quiet for a while. Diara vaguely registered Robbie Williams singing in the background while she loaded their empty plates onto the tray in front of her.

'Xander ...'

'Hmm?' he responded, tipping up his coffee cup to pour the final dregs into his mouth.

'Can I get you some more coffee?'

'No thanks. I think the Americano has raced around and neutralised the Shiraz in my bloodstream.'

'So, no designated driver tonight?'

'No, not tonight,' he said. 'You have taken enough money off me.'

Diara slipped off her shoes and curled her legs under her.

'So how is your family in Zim? Has your mum managed to get bail?'

Diara shook her head and sighed. 'No, nothing much has changed. Rudo is still preparing her defence. The worst thing is, Mum still blames herself for his death. Oh, I know that she hit him, but it was self-defence. She feels that she deserves to be in jail. It's all so black and white for her. She won't talk about her life and the abuse she suffered, even to her lawyer. She says she doesn't want to tarnish his memory.'

Xander could see that her anxiety levels were increasing, and he tried to think of something calming to say but failed. She went on, sounding agitated, 'Can you believe that? I don't know what to do with her. Sometimes I feel like I'm the crazy one.'

'How are your sisters?' he asked, trying to change the subject.

'They're all right, except Shaan, my older sister. She still has nightmares and cries a lot. I suppose that's not surprising, given she was there.'

'When will the trial begin?'

'Rudo thinks it will be more than a year. Probably around fifteen months. Anyway,' she said, taking a deep breath and obviously trying to control her emotions, '*c'est la vie*. We just have to work hard to make sure that Mum gets the lightest possible sentence.' She sighed. 'How is Saskia really doing? Is she recovering from losing the babies?'

Xander took his cue. 'She's hanging in there. She has lots of support from her parents, so that helps. At least she has stopped digging up the bedroom floor looking for the miscarried babies.'

His words made Diara realise how difficult this period had been for him. It also brought a flashback from her childhood, which she immediately repressed.

'And you? How are you?'

Leanne had told Diara that, after she had lost her second baby, Saskia had had an affair with Cecil from their varsity group. He had been Xander's best mate, so that was an added blow. Apparently, Xander had blamed the miscarriages for his wife's behaviour. They were still married and trying to move on. Needless to say, Xander and Cecil were no longer friends.

'I'm doing all right. I guess you just get on. Got no choice.'

They sat in silence for a while, mulling over the information they had shared.

'I've learned more about you this evening than in all the years I've known you.'

'Well, what you don't know about me is that I'm a horrible person. You know what? All I felt was relief when I heard that my father was dead. He was always there, a terrible secret, stopping me from moving forward, getting on with my life. When I got home after Shaan called me, she couldn't stop crying. Ambuya was crying. Mum was more upset about my father dying than she was about being up on a murder charge. And all the time I kept thinking, why are they crying? Thank God we're rid of him!'

'I'm so sorry your mum reacted like that. And your sisters. I don't know why. Maybe they were in shock?'

'Maybe. But in another life, things could have been different. You're the one person I would not reject. When I needed to escape my memories of my father, I went to a happy place in my mind. And you were often in my happy place, doing what you do best: laughing and telling silly jokes.'

Xander looked at her in surprise but said nothing.

She knew she had exposed her soul and he might feel uncomfortable. He'd never been much good at emotional stuff. He was probably wondering what the hell he had got into by meeting her ... She decided to put him out of his misery. 'Don't worry. I promise I'm not a loony or a stalker. Just trying to keep my mental health robust.'

Xander took his cue and laughed. There was a long pause. 'Is that why you don't drink?' he asked suddenly. 'Because of your father?'

'Yes. He put me off completely. I saw too much of the destructive side of it. Also remember that Mum is Muslim – she wouldn't have alcohol in the house. Ironic, isn't it, when her husband was a drunk?'

He shook his head sympathetically. 'Do you realise that if we had spoken as frankly at varsity as we did today, our lives may have taken a different turn?'

'Perhaps. Or maybe we would have burned our bridges early. Maybe we're different people now. Calmer, more able to listen and understand each other's point of view.'

'You're probably right.' Xander checked his watch. It was almost midnight. 'I guess I'd better get going,' he said reluctantly. 'You have an early flight and I have a seven a.m. breakfast meeting.'

'Okay. Let me get the bill,' she said, looking around for the waiter.

'Don't worry, Dee, I've got it.'

'What? But it was my treat!'

'It's too late now. Next time. I promise.'

They stood up and walked into the foyer.

'Let me see you up to your room,' he said as they neared the lifts.

Diara did not protest; she was glad to have a few more minutes with him. As they stepped out of the lift, she turned to him. 'Thanks for listening to my sad story.'

When they stopped outside her room, he looked down at her. 'Are you going to be all right? You will let me know if you need anything or any help with your sisters or mum, won't you?'

'Of course. Thank you.' Unlike the last time, she wanted him to stay. It all felt a bit unfinished. She scrambled in her bag for her key card.

'See you soon?' he asked, raising his eyebrows. 'Summer? We want to come over.'

'Absolutely!' She reached up to rub the cleft in his chin with her thumb and kiss his cheek. Later, thinking back to this moment, she knew that this was when everything started to spiral out of control. As she went to move away, his hand came up and he traced her cheekbone gently. She wasn't even sure if she remembered it correctly, if this was her interpretation of what had happened, or if this was what she'd wanted to happen.

Diara froze. Xander kissed the top of her head. She wasn't sure what to do. The next minute seemed to last forever. She looked up at him. He stroked her hair, which flowed over one shoulder, and twisted it around his hand. 'Gosh,' he said in a surprised voice, 'I have always wanted to do this.' He twisted it further until it was wrapped around his hand. 'You need to tell me to leave,' he said softly, but at the same time he was using his free index finger to trace the outline of her lips.

Diara felt her head and heart pounding. She didn't want to make the decision he was thrusting at her. She just wanted him to go on touching her. *It's okay*, she reassured herself – or fooled herself? *I don't want much. Just one hug.* But her arm crept up his chest and round his neck.

'I don't know if I can do that,' she said, moving closer and laying her head on his chest.

He held her tight. They remained in an embrace for a long time. Diara looked up at him again, despite what the reasonable side of her brain was yelling at her to do.

'You leave if you want. I don't want you to go.'

'Oh, sugar,' he said softly, 'I knew that coming to your

room was a bad idea. But I couldn't stop myself.' He leant down and kissed her gently on the mouth. That ended the conversation. He took her key card, opened the door for her and followed her in. Once in the room, he shut the door.

'We don't have to do this … I don't want you to hate me afterwards. Be absolutely sure, please.'

She turned around from where she stood near the bed after switching on the bedside lamp. 'I'm sure, but I'm not the one who's married.'

'It's up to you. Whatever happens, my feelings for you will remain the same. You decide.'

She walked up to him and took his hands. 'It's okay, Xander. I understand,' she said. 'You can go.'

'I wish to God I was that noble!' Again, he twisted her hair around his hand and gently pulled her closer. Her permission to leave fell by the wayside.

All Diara knew was that it was gentle, and each touch was reverent. There was no talking. No false promises. It was what it was. His gentleness was endless. Her anxiety was soothed away by time and patience. And she was grateful to him – grateful for his understanding. For his extra care at strategic moments, when he responded to her inhibitions and fears with a soft touch and additional attention. It was just how it should be when entering uncharted territory.

✪✪✪

He gathered her close and rubbed her arm. Her head was tucked beneath his chin. She lay on her side, her hand on his chest. It was not awkward. It was marvellous. She couldn't have wished for more. And she was glad it had been with him. She lifted her head and looked at him. Sadly, their perfect night was almost over, but it was hers to keep for as long as she wanted. All the time she had spent dreaming, imagining and hoping – and it had come to pass. She wanted to smile. Forever. For once, she had a story to tell. A superb story. So, she did what she always did in times of uncertainty: she took control to avoid pain and ensure the scenario ended well, and on her terms.

'Ah, is that a smile?' Xander asked her, looking at her with exaggerated fear on his face. 'Phew! For a minute I thought you were trying to find the words to let me down gently.'

'No, not at all. I just wanted to say—'

He covered his face and groaned. 'Oh no, here it comes! Dear Xander, you are a lovely person, but ...'

Diara hugged him tightly. 'Let's not have any post mortems or walks of shame or words of shame, because I don't feel any.'

Xander's hand, which had been stroking her hair, stilled. He lifted her hand from his chest and kissed her palm.

'I do know that you're honourable and have a great sense of responsibility towards your wife. What I want to say is, I want to remember this little bit of time we've had and not ask for anything more.'

'We could at least meet up occasionally.'

'No!' she said heatedly. 'What did you think? That we were going to meet up a couple of times a year, have a fling? Maybe in this very room?'

Once the words were out, she could not retract them as she wanted to when she saw the look of horror on his face.

'Dee, that's not what I meant, and you know it. Didn't we have a lovely dinner? It was so good to talk and just be us.'

'Of course. Forgive me. Let me finish. Please. I don't want to lose your friendship – or whatever we have. The only way we can salvage it is by locking this time away. I'll think about it whenever I feel down. You can do whatever you want with it, but that's all we can have. I don't want to be that woman – one who waits around for you to be free, to throw me crumbs of affection. I have no regrets … because I honestly didn't want to spend the rest of my life wondering if you were good in bed.'

'What the hell?' he exclaimed.

She sat up in bed and looked at him, smiling. 'Please don't tempt me to be your bit on the side. I deserve better. It's time for me to move on with my life. And Xander, do you really want to be the person with a white wife and a coloured bit on the side? Go back to your life, my darling. I will be okay. Honestly.'

Xander remained silent. Everything she had said made sense. He also knew that once Diara made up her mind, there was no changing it. He sat up, scooted closer to her and lifted her chin to kiss her gently. 'And I thought you were going to tell me how special it was for you!'

Diara stared at him for a minute, confused, then burst out laughing. They held each other. Their thoughts were reflected in their sighs and touches. Gentle. Desperate. Gentle.

'Thank you,' she said, absently rubbing his back.

'What for?'

'For making me feel things that I didn't know I was capable of. Thank you for reminding me that I have a heart.'

He kissed her and pulled her closer.

'I see the sun on your back, Xan.'

'Huh?'

'All these years, you have been there. You changed my life. When I felt it was too painful to carry on, I would force myself to go to places with you. Special places. Trou aux Biches? Remember, you took me to Mauritius for my birthday and we had dinner on that beach?'

'And we went snorkelling. The coral was amazing.' He played along.

'I think my best memory was the weekend break we took at Victoria Falls.'

'Really?' he asked.

'Well, I always say that nothing – no picture or postcard – can prepare you for seeing the Falls. They are magnificent.'

'True.'

'How lucky we were to share that moment.'

'It was beautiful. And the high tea we had at the hotel, with the warthogs running around in the enclosure?'

'Stop it, Alexander! You're too good at this. You are making me dream of things I cannot have.'

Overcome with emotion, she climbed onto his lap to hold him closer.

'I don't think you realise how much you helped me. Whenever I thought of you, you helped to calm me. Your presence helped me to fight demons – demons that would have kept me a prisoner of hatred and anger.'

'I-I had no idea. I'm … humbled. I'm glad I could help.' He embraced her.

'Thank you, Xan, for being you. I honestly believe that I'm only alive thanks to you.'

'I'm not sure I deserve that. But thank you.'

He stayed until it was time for her to leave for her flight to London.

7

LONDON, 2008

'Hi Lea, how are you?'

'Dee, I thought you were going to come over for a drink on your way to the airport. Can you still make it?'

'I wish I could, but sorry. I took longer than I thought to organise stuff at the office. I'm packing now. The taxi will be here in half an hour.'

'I've only seen you once since you got back from Zim. And that was when we picked you up from the airport!'

'I know. I know. I miss you too. But it's been so hectic.'

'Well, I'm worried about you. You have to let us help in any way we can.'

'Lea, you always help. You're the one constant in my life. You found Rudo for me, paid her a retainer, and I don't know what else.'

Leanne ignored this last statement. 'Dee, did you forget to mention to me that you saw Xander on your way back from Zim?'

Oh God, thought Diara, caught off guard. 'Oh, I just didn't mention it because I haven't seen you,' she said quickly.

'Well, I was gobsmacked when he messaged to ask how you were. He said he hadn't heard from you since he saw you in Johannesburg.'

'I know. I know. I've just not had a minute. I promise I'll message him in the taxi. Take care, Lea. See you when I get back.'

'When are you back?'

'The retreat is for ten days. I'll be back next weekend.'

'Okay. Well, why don't you come over for dinner on Saturday? Aidan is covering a story, so we can talk.'

'Sounds wonderful. I'd better go, Leanne. Talk soon.'

Diara finished packing and waited for her taxi to arrive. On her way to the airport, she gazed out of the window. It was a grey, drizzly day after a week of incessant rain. She took out her mobile and read the two messages that Xander had sent. One had arrived three days after she had seen him in Johannesburg.

> Hope you arrived safely. Let me know how you are, and if there's anything I can do for your mum and sisters.

Another text had arrived three days ago. Looking at the date of the first text, Diara realised that three weeks had passed since she had met him.

> Hi Diara, please let me know that you are well.

Oh God, she thought, *I am such a bad person*. She had meant to find time to sit down and think of a response that was friendly, superficial and not needy. Well, it was time to do that; there was no putting it off any longer. Diara took out her laptop and began to write a breezy email.

To: Xanderjoubert@ecoweb.co.za

From: dkruger@childfirst.co.uk

Subject: Greetings

Hey Xander,

I am well. Thanks for your messages. It's been so hectic – time has flown by and I hadn't realised till now that it's been three weeks since we saw each other. Forgive my rudeness – especially as you came out to see me at such short notice and we had a wonderful dinner.

I'm in a taxi to Gatwick, on my way to a ten-day retreat for the southern African staff. Sigh! Retreats can be so dull. But the good thing is, it's in Mauritius! London is so grey and dreary that I'm looking forward to the sunshine, if not the work. Can you imagine sitting in paradise and planning all your activities for the next three years? The worst part is calculating the budgets!

Thank you for your kind offer of help. Mum's lawyer has been very efficient but is still struggling to get bail for her. The police have charged her with murder. Apparently, it will take another year – or longer – for the case to be heard. So sadly Mum may have to spend two Christmases in prison.

Enough about me. How are you? Did you get the account you were bidding for?

I'm fine. Thanks for asking. Please don't worry about me. It was so good to see you. Best therapy in the world!

Give my best to Saskia.

Diara

Diara clicked Send and sat back to relax before the taxi dropped her at the British Airways terminal at Gatwick. She was not looking forward to the twelve-hour flight. But it would be good downtime. Time to think – or not think.

On the flight, her mind inadvertently wandered to Xander. She hoped she had managed to reassure him. She didn't want him to worry about her. But she loved the fact that he had bothered to check on her. In her mind, she had released him from any obligations. But knowing him, he was probably feeling conflicted.

Diara hoped that when Xander came to London as planned in the summer, they could have some time together. She had forced herself not to invest too much in their night together. She did this out of fear – fear that he would say he loved Saskia and didn't want to hurt her. Even thinking about him saying that was painful. Maybe now he'd had time to think, he would agree with her. She could not bear for him to make her any false promises.

What Diara would only realise later was that all her plans were about to explode.

8

LONDON, 2008

LEANNE MCKENZIE

Leanne added the finishing touches to her red Thai curry with prawns and vegetables. It was Diara's favourite. She wanted to make a special dinner for her and was really looking forward to seeing her. They'd have the opportunity to discuss everything that had happened since her dad's death. Leanne sighed with compassion for her friend. Like Diara, she only felt happiness at André Kruger's death. He had been violent and cruel – he deserved his untimely death. She had nothing but admiration for Diara's resilience. She had an incredible ability to pick herself up and move forward.

Leanne sighed, gathered up her curly, shoulder-length dark hair and twisted it into a knot at the back of her head. Her olive skin was smooth and held a sheen from the exertion of cooking. Her dark eyes were tilted at the corners. Her full lips were painted their customary letterbox red.

She finished cooking and began to clear the dining table to set it before Diara arrived. Leanne and Aidan lived in a terraced Victorian house on Windermere Avenue in Queen's Park in London. She and Diara felt strongly that it was not chance that they lived here. The main road running through

Queen's Park was called Salusbury Road – very similar to Salisbury, the capital of Rhodesia. These names were changed to 'Harare' and 'Zimbabwe' after independence in 1980. As further support for their theory that the gods had played a part in deciding where they should live, schools and a mosque in the area were founded and supported by Yusuf Islam, formerly known as Cat Stevens. His music had comforted and provided solace to both women – they had all his recordings, knew all the words, and adored every note he had produced. Even though Aidan, Leanne's husband, had owned the house for a few years before they had met, this was their theory: it was not coincidence but thanks to the gods' intervention that they had ended up living here.

Diara lived a five-minute walk away from Leanne on Chevening Road. Leanne had hounded estate agents in the area looking for accommodation nearby that was suitable for her friend. The hounding had paid off. Leanne had secured the lease on a two-bedroom apartment in a converted Victorian house. The women wanted to be close to one another. The flat was also convenient for Diara's work – a thirty-minute Tube ride to Barbican, where Child First's office was.

Leanne had moved to London two years before Diara, after marrying Aidan Kavanagh, a foreign correspondent for the BBC World News posted in Zimbabwe. He had been recalled to London, and the week before he was due to leave, they decided to marry so that Leanne could join him. Leanne's mum had a few days to arrange the wedding, which was memorable for its tasteful simplicity. It was held in the beautiful gardens of the family home. Leanne's wedding was the first time Diara had met Xander's wife. They had flown up to attend the festivities, along with other varsity friends. After dinner, Diara was in the kitchen with Mrs McKenzie when Xander came in.

'So, how are you? You look amazing, by the way. Dance?' he said, taking in her silver catsuit and high ponytail. They had only been on the dance floor a few minutes when a slow song came on. Xander pulled her closer and they swayed to the beautiful sounds of Led Zeppelin singing 'Stairway to Heaven'. Just as Diara began to relax, they were interrupted by Saskia.

'There you are, Alexander. I couldn't find you. Had you forgotten that I don't really know anyone here?'

Oh God! What an idiot! Diara had pulled herself together.

'Dance with your wife, Xander. She's lonely.'

She'd left them and joined Leanne and Aidan on the dance floor, putting Saskia out of her mind.

✪✪✪

After the wedding, Aidan had left for London and begun the process of applying for Leanne's spouse visa. It took three months. Leanne left a week later. Diara had found it difficult to imagine living in Zimbabwe without Leanne, and had been quiet and withdrawn since the wedding.

Leanne had noticed this. The day before her flight, she turned up at the Child First offices and suggested lunch. They went to a bistro nearby.

'Dee, I am going to miss you terribly. Who will I tell all my deep, dark secrets to?'

'We can talk on the phone. Whenever I have something I want to tell you, I will make a note of it. That way I won't forget. You do the same.'

'Dearest, will you be okay? I wish I could take you with me.' Leanne looked at Diara, her face concerned.

'I'm not sure Aidan would approve of that.'

'We're not asking for his approval, my darling.' They laughed, but it sounded forced.'You know, I was thinking

83

last night that we have never been separated by oceans and deserts.'

'I know ... I love you. I will miss you too.' Emotion welled up in Diara.

'That will never change. Will you look after Mum and Dad for me?'

Diara nodded.

Leanne had made Diara promise to come and visit after she had settled down.

Diara had come over six months later for a two-week summer holiday. The two weeks that she spent with Leanne highlighted how lonely they had been. Diara had lost the only person she trusted; her life felt empty. Even though Leanne had been consumed by the practicalities of immigrating, finding work and carving a new life with Aidan, she'd missed Diara terribly. Her mind would often stray to times she had spent with Diara. She'd missed being able to glance at her friend and know that she understood whatever she wished to communicate with no need for words. During Diara's summer holiday, the friends had decided that they had to find a way to be together again.

❂❂❂

Leanne heard the buzzer and went to open the front door for her friend. 'Hi, Dee! Get in here quickly. It's freezing.'

The friends embraced warmly. 'I can't believe it's been more than a month since I saw you. How are you feeling? I was so disappointed that you couldn't come over last weekend. Come and sit down. What would you like to drink?'

'Nothing, thanks. I have my water. How's Aidan?' Diara took off her coat and hung it on the coat hook near the front door. She walked through to the lounge, listening to her friend chattering.

'He's good. He hasn't had the winter blues yet. Thank God! He's playing football tonight but should be back later. How are you? Any better? Was it a tummy bug?'

'Something like that.'

Leanne suddenly realised that something was wrong with Diara. She turned to look at her friend and noticed that she wore no eyeliner. Just as Leanne would never leave the house without lipstick, it was unheard-of for Diara not to put on eyeliner. She looked pale and exhausted. Leanne finished pouring her wine, then sat down opposite her friend. 'So, what's going on? Are you still poorly?'

'Not really. I'm pregnant.'

Leanne's shock was written all over her face. 'I was not expecting you to say that.'

'I know,' said Diara wryly. 'I'm still trying to get my teeth around it myself.' Her bravado faded towards the end of the sentence and her voice wobbled.

Leanne moved to sit by her friend. 'It's okay, Dee. We will work it all out.' She put her arm around Diara, who was shaking. She soothed her and rubbed her back, utterly confused. She didn't even know that Diara had been seeing anyone.

'Dearest, do we know who the father is?'

Diara nodded and looked at her friend, a trifle more composed but still fragile.

'Do you like him enough to keep the baby? You do know that you don't have to have the baby ...'

Another nod. More tears. 'I can't have an abortion. I tried. I went to the clinic, spoke to the doctor. But I can't do it. It's Mum's Muslim brainwashing, I'm afraid.'

'Okay, so abortion is not an option. So what's the problem? I know you always wanted to have a baby, so why not now?'

'Lea, it's not so simple. I've made a huge mistake. I don't know what I was thinking. It was the relief, I think – the relief that I could be an ordinary woman. That I didn't have to always feel dirty.' More sobs followed.

'I don't understand.'

'Xander is the dad ...'

'Xander ...' Realisation dawned. 'Oh.'

The friends sat in silence for a long while. Leanne gulped down her wine, put down her glass and embraced her friend. Diara leant against her and said nothing.

'And you're sure you want to keep the baby?' Leanne asked the million-dollar question softly.

Diara nodded.

'Are you going to tell Xander?'

Diara became agitated and pushed her hair away from her face. 'No, I don't think so ... No.'

'Okay, let's start from the beginning. Tell me all about it.'

So Diara told her about her visit to Johannesburg to see Xander and everything that had happened there. At the end, Leanne sighed. 'Well. I don't know what to say. I want to say that I'm glad you finally told him how you feel. And from what you're saying, you parted on good terms. You don't think that Xander deserves to know?'

'I don't know. I go to his town, invite him to dinner, invite him to my room and tell him my whole sad tale. Next thing, we're in bed. Am I really going to phone him a month later and say "Guess what? You knocked me up! Congratulations!"'

'That's harsh. I'm sure it wasn't as calculated as that.'

'Maybe not, but it doesn't look good. He's married and they're battling to have a baby. The last thing I want is for him to feel that I manipulated him or used him. I don't want to be the cause of any more problems for him.'

'First, I think that the problems were already there, well before you went to Jo'burg. Second, there's always been something between the two of you, so telling him that must have felt powerful for you. Third, Xander is not stupid or weak. He wanted to be with you. Also, it doesn't sit well with me that you don't want to tell him about his baby. Don't you think he deserves to know?'

'Maybe. Let me think it through. I'm so confused and I feel sick to the pit of my stomach. What keeps going around in my head is, does this poor child deserve me as a mother?' She burst into tears again after having shared her biggest fear with her friend. 'You know how fucked up I am, Lea. I'm crazy. I don't want this baby to have to live through what I have.'

'The fact that you recognise that you want your child to grow up in a healthier environment is really important here. I believe that you can provide that – despite what you think. Come on, Diara, this is Xander – the only man you've ever wanted. Are you really going to hurt his child? Get real.'

'I asked him, you know. Asked him why he didn't ask me out at varsity. He admitted that it was because I wasn't white, and my demeanour put him off. I was too stand-offish.'

Leanne could see this degenerating into a circular argument. 'Let's have dinner. We can talk more later.'

'I want you to promise me that you won't tell him.'

Leanne hesitated. 'Look, my loyalty is always with you. I promise, but I want it on record that I don't agree.'

'Lea …'

'Yes?'

'I can't face seafood of any sort.'

Leanne burst out laughing and the friends hugged.

'What do you feel like? Toast?'

Aidan arrived home as the friends were finishing dinner. He was a beautiful, brash, black-haired, blue-eyed Irishman who was the heart of any gathering. 'Hello, beautiful ladies. It is fierce weather out there.' He hugged his wife from behind as she sat in her chair, and kissed the top of her head. 'How are you, Diara? Back from whatever exotic place you were visiting?'

Diara smiled and turned around to hug him. Her eyes were red and she felt nauseous.

'So ... what's been going on?' he asked, looking curious.

'We're having a baby,' said his wife, smiling at Diara. Diara smiled back, knowing Leanne's love of drama.

Aidan's shocked face was a pleasure to behold. He stared at his wife in terror. 'I need a drink,' he gasped, pouring himself some wine and gulping it down. 'I thought that was an adventure you and I were not considering in this lifetime.'

'We're not,' said Leanne, putting him out of his misery. 'Diara is.'

'Oh, thank the Lord!' he said with hysterical relief. 'You sure put the heart crossways in me!'

❂❂❂

When they were getting ready for bed after Diara had left, Aidan broached the subject of the baby. 'Spill, my darling. Which brave man has managed to get our Diara up the duff?'

'Aidan! That's disgusting! I hate that expression.'

He slid into bed, watching her as she hung up her clothes. 'Ah, come on, do tell. Married couples shouldn't have secrets,' he said, winking.

She knew she would tell him everything – he was a

master at squeezing secrets out of her. He had to know – she didn't want him to mention Diara's pregnancy to Xander. 'I'm going to tell you, even though you're a professional gossipmonger posing as a journalist. But I can only tell you if you promise not to tell anyone.'

'Why?' He looked surprised. 'Oh God, it's not Tony Blair, is it? He laughed raucously.

'Listen, if I tell you, you have to promise to keep it to yourself. You especially cannot tell the father.'

'Aha, more and more mysterious.' She took her time getting into bed, rubbing hand cream into her arms and hands excruciatingly, painfully slowly.

'Come on, love, it's not the fucking Pope! It's our Diara.'

His wife finally gave in and put him out of his misery. She explained the events leading up to the pregnancy.

'Well, I can't say I'm surprised. Those two have never been comfortable with each other. I thought maybe they had a past, but now it sounds like they didn't. They obviously have the hots for each other, though. Also, you two treat his wife like dirt. It all makes sense now.'

His wife glared at him as he lay in bed, his hands behind his back.

'What do you expect, Aidan? She's so bloody entitled and patronising. I felt like he had slapped us in the face when he married her. It felt as if we didn't know him at all. At the wedding, after I met her, I thought I was in a Monty Python sketch. She's convinced she's not racist because she has a brown friend and volunteers at a flipping homeless shelter. There were only two people of colour at their wedding. Diara didn't bother to go.'

'Look, I get it, but it's wrong not to tell him.'

'Absolutely, my darling, but it's not our secret to tell. We have to respect that.'

'I hate to warn you, but this is gonna come back to bite us all,' he said sleepily, switching off his lamp and snuggling up to his wife.

She lay awake for a long time, her mind buzzing. She was nervous about keeping Diara's secret. It was going to affect her relationship with Xander – at so many levels.

9

FARISH

It's only when you have a big old secret that you realise how small the world really is. So much had happened in the last few months that Diara found she appreciated quiet time in her flat more than anything else. She just went out to work, did enough shopping to survive and had dinner each week at Leanne's.

Leanne had failed to convince her to tell Xander about the baby. But thankfully, she'd given up lecturing her on the rights of fathers to know their children. In her mind, Diara was making the best of a bad situation. A situation of her own making. She didn't want to drag Xander into her family's sordid business or put him in a situation where he was conflicted and had to choose between two women. In her view, getting pregnant by him during a one-night stand would make her unpopular in the eyes of the world. In contrast, Saskia, the poor wife who was struggling to conceive, would come out looking angelic and wholesome. She knew how bad it looked. It was most likely that Xander would stay with his wife. And why not? She was his wife. So, rather than having to go through the pain of finding out how he would react, she decided it was easier not to tell him. She would – as she usually did when faced with a difficult situation – leave it to the gods and see what happened.

Of course, what she really wanted was to have him with her, looking forward to the baby. But that was not going to happen. So she was grateful to have Leanne and Aidan. They took turns to go to midwife appointments with her, helped her to shop for everything the baby would need, and spent hours helping to change Diara's second bedroom into a nursery.

Back in Zimbabwe, Sophia had not yet been granted bail. Every month, when the case came up for remand, no trial date was set. At first the delay was due to the police not having completed their investigation. Once they had, the delay was due to a backlog of cases. Sophia's case was remanded to the following month. Rudo was considering an application to the high court for bail. But the chance of it being granted was slim.

Dear Diara,

The State vs Sophia Kruger

I am writing to give you an update. I have not been able to secure bail for Sophia, but I will persevere. However, she is as well as can be expected. I use the money you send for her every month to take her food that fits in with her dietary requirements. I am not sure yet whether I am going to call her as a witness. She is unwilling to talk about the violence she suffered at the hands of your father, and that could harm her defence case.

Second, I have managed to track down Mandy Kaputa. She is still at the University of Zimbabwe Medical School. I have had an initial meeting with her, but she is very reluctant to talk about your case except to confirm that you were at one time a patient. When I asked her specific questions, she said she could not answer without discussing it with you first. As you know, while she is bound generally by patient/client confidentiality, in terms of the law, confidentiality protections do not apply when the information is about the threat or commission of a criminal act. Could you perhaps email her? I think she would welcome your reassurance that she may share with the court some of your case file.

She did say that you were in the strongest position to help your mother by giving evidence. I'm not sure what she meant, and she would not elaborate. Could I remind you of the conversation we had when you were last in Zimbabwe about how conviction rates and sentences the world over show clearly that legal systems do not show empathy to women who kill their husbands, no matter what they may have done? And Zimbabwe is no exception.

So I am concerned. Your mother is refusing to say that her husband regularly almost beat her to death. I would like to go to court confident that I know everything there is to know about your father and his family. So again I stress, if there is anything you can tell me that can assist your mother, now is the time.

I would like you to draft a statement about the domestic violence you saw or suffered. Try to include as many incidents as you can remember, but please be specific.

How old were you?

What was the trigger? For example, after your mother was beaten because the food was cold.

Injuries sustained by you or anyone else. Did the injuries require medical attention? If they did, can you remember the doctor/hospital where medical treatment was given?

Who else witnessed the incident?

Did you tell anyone about the incident? Who did you tell, and was any action taken? Is the person you told able to be contacted?

I have met Shaan and asked her to do the same. Shaan is still finding it difficult to discuss your dad's death. I suggest that she would benefit from some counselling sessions. I could ask Mandida. I think the sessions would better prepare her to give evidence. However, I don't know whether I will call her to the stand – I don't wish to traumatise her again, and the quality and credibility of her evidence may be negatively impacted by her responses.

Finally, as I said earlier, asking Sophia to give testimony may not be a useful strategy. She insists that she cannot talk about her 'home life' in public and she deserves to be punished for taking your father's life. I have failed to get any information from her that could assist in her defence. So I have hired a psychologist who works for a local organisation that provides services to victims of domestic violence. I hope that she has the skills and experience to build a relationship with Sophia. Depending on the information she gathers, it may be more useful to call her to give evidence to the court instead of Sophia.

After reading the email several times, Diara realised that she had little choice. She sent an email to Mandida. She then began to draft a statement. It took her more than two weeks of painfully opening memory boxes she had locked away so they wouldn't affect her present life.

Xander and Saskia visited London for a two-week holiday in June. Diara was at the beginning of her third trimester. The baby's due date was 4 August. She knew she could not meet Xander, because her bump was too difficult to disguise. He had messaged Leanne and Diara suggesting that all five of them get together for dinner. In addition, he had emailed Diara suggesting that they meet for coffee. Diara had been grateful that she could truthfully tell him that she would be attending various meetings in preparation for the United Nations General Assembly in New York, so they would have to meet for coffee another time. It was her last work assignment before she would be too pregnant to fly.

❊❊❊

On 8 August, Diara gave birth to her son. She had been in labour for fourteen hours. Leanne was with her all the time. Finally, her son arrived. He was eight pounds and some ounces and had his mother's black hair.

Leanne went home to rest, but Diara was too excited to sleep. She spent hours staring at her baby, finding it difficult to believe that she was a mother.

Leanne returned later with her famous butternut and sweet potato soup. She sat on a chair by the bed and held the baby while Diara ate her soup.

'He asked about you, you know?'

'Leanne – don't, please. We've been over this.'

'I know. I know. He asked if you were well and what was happening about your mum. He then asked if you were avoiding him. So I said you really were in New York and why would you avoid him? He laughed and said that he didn't believe I didn't know why.'

'What did you say?'

'I told him he was crazy and changed the subject. I didn't want to discuss it with him – or listen to what he was about to say.'

'Why?'

'Because I didn't want him to know that I know that you two hooked up. I don't want to feel even worse that I haven't told him about his baby.'

'I'm sorry, Lea. I really am. It was a difficult decision for me too. I know if I had told him, he would be in a terrible position. His marriage would be destroyed and he would be forced to support a baby he never planned for with a woman he hardly knows.'

'I know you're sorry, and I understand where you're coming from. But I still feel bad. Look, Dee, I don't pretend to understand your relationship with Xander – it was always weird. You guys should have scratched that itch years ago.'

Diara burst out laughing. 'Don't be ridiculous, Leanne. That was the last thing on his mind.'

Leanne rolled her eyes. Diara was always blind to emotional stuff that was staring her in the face.

'The sad thing is that seeing Xander has led to other things, things that torture me.'

Her friend looked at her, concerned. 'Like what, my darling?'

'It's like a part of me that was frozen is slowly thawing. Even worse, I can't bear to think that he's somewhere in the world but without me and the baby. Before, I accepted that he preferred other women to me, but now the stupid baby hormones have muddled my brain and taken away my defences.'

The friends were silent for a while, lost in their thoughts.

'So, have you decided what you're going to call the baby?'

'Yes. Farish. I remember it from the book of Malaysian fairy stories Mum used to read to us. I looked up the meaning recently – it said "knight".'

'Oh, that's an interesting name. Sounds lovely!'

They looked at each other and burst out laughing.

'By the way, did you notice that Farish has blue eyes?' Leanne asked.

'Yes. What are the odds of that? It must be a combination of genes from my dad's side and Xander's. Hopefully, eye colour is all my baby will inherit from that man.'

Diara took her baby home the next day. She was grateful for Leanne's help. Leanne had taken three days off work. She would mind Farish during the day, giving Diara the opportunity to nap. Farish woke up almost every hour at night and by morning she was shattered. The day Leanne went back to work, Diara had never felt so alone in her life. Leanne came by in the evening with food and, after making sure that she had eaten, urged her to lie down. But Diara found it hard to relax: her senses were hypervigilant because she was listening out for Farish.

So, when the midwife arrived the next morning to do a routine check, Diara felt tears threatening at her kind inquiries. Farish was screaming for milk and Diara tried to feed him without wincing. Her nipples were red-raw and swollen.

'It's hard work, isn't it?' the midwife said sympathetically. 'Do you have anyone to help you with baby?'

'My friend, Leanne – she comes in the evenings with dinner and helps me to bath Farish.'

'So, is the father not in the picture?'

'No … um … he does not know.'

'Right. Let me examine you and check all is well, then we can decide what to do.'

Farish had dozed off, so Diara put him down and allowed herself to be examined. During the examination, Farish was awake again and fussing. The midwife put him over her shoulder and soothed him. 'Look, I don't think you're producing enough milk for the baby – that's why he's fussy and feeds so often. From what I saw, you have got the hang of feeding and baby latches on well.'

Diara nodded. 'He gets frustrated after a few minutes.'

'He has lost some weight. But that's normal. More importantly, do you want to breastfeed? It's not something that every woman is comfortable with or wants to do.'

'I want to, but I have some hang-ups about it. I grew up in Africa. Most African women are comfortable breastfeeding in public, but I guess I never got used to the idea of it.'

'Well, you don't have to do it. I see that you have been on medication in the past for depression.'

'Yes, when I was fifteen, for a short while.'

'In other circumstances, I would say let's wait a week or so for your milk to come in, but I don't want you to get sad or down because of breastfeeding difficulties. Let's make some tea and talk about it.' The midwife bustled into the kitchen.

Sitting at the table with tea, they discussed the midwife's plan. 'There are some supplements that assist milk production, such as fennel, fenugreek, thistle and dates. But you also have to drink enormous amounts of water with them. So I suggest a large packet of salted nuts to increase your thirst.'

'What about my nipples? They're so painful – I am sure that Farish feels my pain.'

'I suggest that we try fennel tea and nipple shields for a week. The nipple shields will allow you to heal.'

Diara felt a sense of relief. She smiled and nodded.

'Good. Let me speak to your friend on the phone. Would she be willing to stop at the pharmacy to pick up your prescription on her way home from work?'

'Of course.'

'Good. I'll do that now. I can hear baby stirring but, before you fetch him, I wondered if there was anything else that was causing you stress. Stress has a way of affecting milk production. If there is anything you're worried about, you can tell me about it.'

Diara rang Leanne and left her to speak to the midwife. Picking up her son, she rocked him and sang to him softly. As she breathed in his baby smell, she realised it was the best smell in the world. She lay down on her bed to feed him. When she woke up, Leanne was standing next to her, smiling and holding a mug of aromatic fennel tea. Diara had no idea when the midwife had left.

Over supper, while they were discussing the midwife's visit, Leanne suddenly picked up her phone. 'Let's phone Xander.'

Diara gulped. 'Why?' she managed to whisper.

'Talk to him, dearest. See if you can tell him.' She scrolled down, looking for his number.

Diara leapt up, on the pretext of checking on Farish. She stood staring down at him. She could hear Leanne talking to Xander on the phone. She clutched the edge of his Moses basket.

'Dee, Xan is on the phone.'

She walked back to the table, her movements robotic, and took the phone. 'Hey, Xander.'

'Dee! Are you okay? It's been a long time.' He sounded happy.

'Fine. Fine. And you?'

'All good. What news from your mum?'

They discussed possible court dates. All the while, her heart was racing. How could she tell him?

'Diara? Dee.'

She realised she had not heard his last question.

'Xan … um … will you be coming over to the UK soon?'

He was silent. 'Dee, is anything wrong? You're not sick?'

'No. No. I'm good. There was just something I wanted to talk to you about.'

'Hello, Diara!' She heard Saskia's voice in the background.

All her good intentions fell by the wayside. 'But it's not urgent.' She ignored Saskia. Leanne was looking at her sympathetically. She realised her cheeks were wet.

'Dee?' There was concern in his voice.

'Talk soon, Xan.' She hung up.

Leanne came over to hug her. 'It's okay, dearest. Small steps. Soon you will manage.'

Diara decided to bring up something that had been bothering her for a while. 'Lea, listen. I don't want you to lie to Xander by omission any more. I shouldn't have asked you to do that. If you are in a situation where you are unable to lie to him, please do what you feel is right. You have always put me first in your life, and I know you would never do anything to harm me.'

Later, after Leanne had left, she took a picture of Farish sleeping and sent it to Rudo, with a request that she ring Diara the next time she went to visit her mum in prison. Diara knew it was time she told her mum about Farish. Once she had told her mum, then she would tell her sisters.

❁❁❁

It took a couple of months, but eventually breastfeeding became easier. The supplements and the health visitor's advice helped. One morning, Diara woke up and realised she only had a week of maternity leave left. The six months had flown past. Although she could extend her maternity leave to a year, she was reluctant to do this as it would mean a reduced salary, and she needed her full salary as she was sending money home to Zimbabwe. Then she heard from Rudo that her mum's case was due to be heard in a few months, so she would need leave to go there and give evidence. She quickly got out of bed and dressed. Farish was going to nursery. She fed him quickly, then grabbed his changing bag and the bottles of milk she had expressed.

Leanne had found a nursery nearby which they had both liked. Farish was starting there a week before Diara had to go back to work, so he had time to get used to the new setting. Once she had dropped him off, she was nervous. Back home, she was restless and called the nursery four times to check on him.

Child First paid for school fees and childcare fees as a perk for their permanent staff. They also gave breastfeeding staff members the option to come to work an hour later and leave an hour earlier, or whatever suited them. When Diara returned to work, she soon established a routine but clock-watched all day until it was time to rush to the nursery to fetch her baby.

10

HARARE, 2009

Sophia's trial was scheduled to take place at the high court in Harare. It was estimated to take five days. Diara had been correct in her prediction that her mum would have two Christmases in prison on remand before her trial. It was eighteen months since her father had died. Farish was already seven months old. Time had flown by for her – but not, she imagined, for her mum.

She travelled to Harare with Farish, where she was met by all three sisters. Her sisters' reaction to her baby was adorable. They vied for his attention – and he loved it. He probably could not believe that he had so many ladies whose hair he could pull. However, his heart lay firmly with Ambuya. They were fascinated by each other. As soon as Ambuya spoke to him in her lyrical, accented English, a smile would break out on his face, although her conversation was limited to 'Hello my pretty, pretty boy!' What he loved most was when she tied him on her back with a towel, in the traditional African way, for a nap. She would go about her chores with him tied to her back, singing him Shona hymns.

Rudo had taken Diara to visit Sophia in prison the afternoon before the trial was set to begin. Farish was with them, although he had fallen asleep in the car. Despite this,

Sophia sat with the baby in her lap, happily staring at him. 'You are really a mother, Deedee.' She lapsed into Afrikaans – a language she was obviously more comfortable with. Diara, however, responded in English. Although she understood Afrikaans, her ability to speak it was very limited.

'*Hy is baie mooi.*' He is very beautiful. '*Die Pa?*' The father?

'Mum, you haven't met him.'

'Is he going to marry you?' she asked, reverting to English.

'No, Mum. The question should be, am I going to marry him?'

'You must, Deedee! It's *haram* not to!' Sophia was referring to activities that are forbidden and unlawful in the Muslim religion, such as eating pork. Diara rolled her eyes at her mother.

'Mum, let's not discuss my lack of a husband now, please. Can we talk about court tomorrow?'

'No, we can't,' her mother replied. 'You are ruining my first time with my grandson. I have already told you that I'm not saying anything in court. I have made my peace with God. Humans can judge me as they want. I don't care.'

Rudo placed a folder before her client. Sophia did not bother to look at it. 'Sophia, I am required by law to provide you with certain documentation before the trial begins tomorrow.' Rudo removed all the papers in the folder. 'This one outlines the details of the charge against you, and the date and notice of trial. This is a list of the witnesses that the prosecution will call. There is a summary of evidence that each witness will give. This will give you an idea of the case against you. Finally, this is an outline of my defence, a list of witnesses I will call, and a summary of the evidence that each one will give. Shall we go through them together?'

Sophia looked up from Farish and shook her head. 'No. I will read through it all after you have gone.'

'Are you sure, Mum?' Diara asked disbelievingly.

'Yes.'

Rudo looked from mother to daughter and quickly intervened. 'You do that, Sophia. I will be back at five thirty to discuss everything with you.'

❂❂❂

Rudo showed Diara, Ambuya and the baby to separate rooms. Witnesses giving evidence were not allowed in the courtroom during the trial and they were banned from speaking to each other, to minimise the possibility of collaboration and collusion. Witnesses could not hear any other testimony which could affect their own. During the scheduled trial period, the prosecution would try to prove murder by showing that Sophia had the necessary criminal intention and had planned to kill her husband. The defence, on the other hand, would try to prove her innocence: Sophia had acted in self-defence, since she had been in imminent fear for her life.

The public prosecutor had a list of three witnesses. This appeared to be because the prosecution case was dependent on Sophia's confession. There was no disagreement between the sides over what and who had caused André's death.

The first witness was the medical examiner who had conducted the post mortem on André, and the second was the police officer who had collected all the evidence and prepared the file for the prosecution. The third witness was Ambuya, who had been interviewed by the police about the events of that night. Ambuya told Diara that she had been warned not to discuss her statement with anyone, as had all the witnesses.

Rudo, in her pre-trial meeting with the prosecutor, had been adamant that there was no point calling Shaan to give evidence. They had decided that, although Shaan had been first on the scene, André was already on the floor, bleeding. She was not going to contribute anything new to their case, as she had not been present during the events that led to his death. Rudo was relieved that Shaan was not required to take the stand. She felt that any information she needed about the Krugers' family life could be provided by Diara and other witnesses in their testimony.

Shaan was still very fragile. The trauma of being first on the scene, seeing her father lying in a pool of blood and her mother taken away by the police, had left her with emotional scars. Rudo was concerned that the prosecution would exploit her vulnerability. Diara, on the other hand, in Rudo's opinion, had a courage born from distancing herself from the situation emotionally and physically. In the end, Rudo had called four witnesses to provide evidence on behalf of the defence. They were Dr Davidzo Hatendi, Diara, Dr Mandida Kaputa and Dr Inviolata Marimo. Dr Hatendi was a doctor who collaborated with a private investigation company. In a former life he had been employed by the government medical examiner's office. He had left to return to private practice as a general practitioner. However, he was often called to court to provide a second opinion as an expert witness in court cases. Diara would give evidence after him, mostly through the witness statement she had prepared. Dr Mandida Kaputa had treated Diara as a teen, and Dr Inviolata Marimo was a psychologist who would be giving her report on her assessment of Sophia. She was an expert in the field of domestic violence and worked for a local non-governmental agency supporting survivors of violence.

Rudo sat at the defence table, waiting for her client to be brought in. She grimaced on recalling her meeting yesterday evening with Sophia. The only comment Sophia had made about the paperwork Rudo had left for her was: 'Wasn't it kind of Diara to exaggerate her story to protect me?' Rudo shook her head.

The prosecution had to prove to the court, beyond reasonable doubt, that Sophia had had an actual criminal intention to kill André. Rudo was relatively confident that they would find it difficult to prove this. She smiled to herself as she thought about the prosecution trying to prove that Sophia was malicious and spiteful enough to plan to kill André. That certainly wasn't the Sophia she knew, the Sophia who blamed herself for all her husband's wrongs.

Rudo's thoughts were interrupted by Sophia's arrival. She stood up as two policewomen led Sophia to the table. She was dressed in the black dress that Diara had brought her yesterday. Today, she was wearing a white scarf and was holding her prayer beads.

After checking on Sophia, Rudo looked around the room. She noticed that the court policeman was allowing members of the public to enter the courtroom. She recognised some faces: there were a few human rights activists, lawyers and court reporters. She was gratified by the turnout. She hoped that this case would be an important landmark in highlighting domestic violence.

Criminal matters in the high court in Zimbabwe are heard by a judge and two assessors. Assessors are usually retirees from different fields, including media and education. The two assessors assist in making findings on factual issues only and have an equal say with the judge in relation to the facts. The judge in Sophia's trial was in his late fifties and had been appointed to the bench two years earlier. Rudo had not been pleased when she heard that this judge had been allocated to her case. She wondered how sensitive he was to issues of gender-based violence. Judge Innocent Chanetsa had yet to hear a case where domestic violence was one of the factors leading to a murder. Did he believe that women had the right to live in a home free of violence? That was difficult to assess. Rudo had implied to Diara that it was possible that the judge, having lived in a patriarchal society in which polygamy was acceptable, might not find it unreasonable to chastise a wife for being 'disobedient'. However, there was nothing they could do about it; they would just have to hope for a fair trial. Another thorn in Rudo's side was the public prosecutor. Panashe Mafuta was a chief law officer in the Department of Public Prosecutions. He was ten years younger than the judge, had an exceptionally good record of convictions, and was good-looking and arrogant. She had battled with him in court twice before and had had a difficult time maintaining her calm.

Everyone stood up and waited for the judge and his entourage to be seated. Sophia stood up but did not look up or around her. She continued to fiddle with her beads. The prosecution gave his opening remarks. His address was brief but had an impact.

'Your Honour, Sophia Kruger killed her husband with cold-hearted intent. She lay in bed and waited for him to return from his night out, and when he was at his most vulnerable, used a blunt, heavy object to hit him, resulting in his death. We have evidence from the forensic medical examiner regarding the nature of Mr Kruger's injuries and how they were inflicted, which will support our argument that Sophia Kruger planned to murder her husband.

'The investigating officer in this case will give evidence about the crime scene when he arrived at Mr Kruger's home on the fateful night. Finally, the housekeeper at the Kruger home will give evidence about the nature of the Kruger marriage. She will show a pattern of behaviour whereby Sophia was disrespectful and hostile to her husband. This will show her in her true light.

'The defence, on the other hand, will paint her as a victim – a victim of domestic violence who, allegedly, was regularly beaten by the deceased. However, why did Mrs Kruger not mention these beatings to anyone? The police have no record of anyone reporting domestic violence at the Kruger home. Contrary to this, we have actual evidence that Mrs Kruger would goad the victim and deliberately disobey him, which resulted in marital conflict. She was the instigator.

'André also had an eye for the ladies. This was the last straw for Sophia. She could not control his amorous behaviour, so she formed the intention to kill him and planned how and when she was going to do it. She succeeded in her plot. This was simply an act of revenge: she succeeded in eliminating a womanising husband who was out of her control. Your Honour, the prosecution will prove the necessary *mens rea* or actual intent on the part of Sophia Kruger to kill her husband, André Kruger, the victim.'

How unusual, Rudo thought, legalising assault for his convenience. She stood up and began her opening remarks, which were just as brief but had a different twist.

'Your Honour, the prosecution will endeavour to convince you that Mr Kruger had a minor part to play in his untimely death. They will portray a simple story of a man who was forced to beat his wife – she invited the beatings by behaving in a certain manner, by not obeying him and by disrespecting him. Please note, Your Honour, that in the prosecution's opening argument Mrs Kruger, the accused, is blamed for these beatings. My learned friend has already set the scene for the prosecution's case by legalising assault to justify his theory that Mrs Kruger was a bad woman, which is why she got beaten. She provoked poor, innocent Mr Kruger. This is what I am hearing. Further, he romanticised Mr Kruger's adulterous behaviour by referring to it "as an eye for the ladies" and "amorous behaviour".

'Well, at this point let me leave you with the picture of Mr and Mrs Kruger painted by the prosecution. It is simplistic and unrealistic. The defence is going to give a more complex, realistic assessment of the situation at the Kruger home. It is not a naïve, one-dimensional picture of a venomous, nagging wife and a long-suffering husband forced to find comfort with other women. And then look what happened – the nagging wife who loves to be beaten finally killed him! Poor Mr Kruger! Unfortunately, there are so many more layers to this story. Sophia Kruger was a battered woman. We will hear expert evidence from the psychologist who has worked with her during her incarceration. I would like to show you that it was very reasonable for Sophia to fear for her life. She had been doing that for most of her married life.

'It is time for the law and the courts to recognise the complexity of human relationships. The defence is going to unveil much more of the situation in the Kruger home that culminated in the death of Mr Kruger: unpalatable secrets and unpunished crimes. Professionals will give evidence of the constraints the women and the children in the Kruger home faced daily. Your Honour, we look forward to taking you on an alternative journey, one that has more texture and depth than the simple notions of the prosecution. Our evidence will show the violence suffered by the Kruger women at the hands of Mr Kruger. In fact, by the time we have finished, we are sure that the picture painted by the prosecution will have been eliminated from your mind.'

Following the opening arguments, the prosecution called the medical examiner to give evidence on the injuries that had caused Mr Kruger's death. Dr Mahere took the stand. Despite the heat in the courtroom, he wore a three-piece suit and a white shirt. His tie was neatly knotted, and he periodically mopped his face with a white handkerchief. He answered the questions put forward by the prosecution precisely. It was obvious that giving evidence in murder trials was something he had done many times. Dr Mahere only answered the questions asked. He did not elaborate unless he was specifically asked to follow up a question. The medical examiner's findings were not complicated or in dispute. Dr Mahere confirmed that the victim had died from blunt force trauma to the head, as everyone had suspected. The traumatic brain injury had been caused by the heavy, carved malachite lamp which had been on a bedside table in the room in which the victim was found. The lamp was provided by the prosecution as Exhibit 1.

Rudo examined the lamp when it was passed to her. Like most Zimbabwean sculptures, it was beautiful in its simplicity. It was carved in the shape of a mother carrying her child on her back, secured in a wrap. It was made of dark green malachite and emphasised the mother–child bond in a very expressive manner.

Dr Mahere went on to say that the lamp had been identified by the police officer as the murder weapon, and this had been confirmed by the accused. In addition, the murder weapon had had traces of blood and bone from Mr Kruger's skull on it. The blow had caused maximum damage because the corner of the base of the lamp had come into contact with the victim's skull, so all the force was concentrated in that small area. The blow had resulted in an epidural haematoma, which was described as bleeding between the tough tissue lining the inside of the skull and the skull itself. The doctor also advised the court that blood tests showed that the victim's alcohol levels were four times above the legal limit to drive.

Rudo had a few questions for the doctor in cross-examination. 'Dr Mahere, how much do you think the murder weapon weighs?'

'It weighs approximately two and a half kilograms.'

'Dr Mahere, how much do you think Mrs Kruger weighs?'

The doctor looked at Sophia then responded. 'I would hazard a guess that she weighs approximately one hundred and ten pounds.'

'Very good guess, Dr Mahere – she weighs one hundred and fifteen pounds or fifty-two kilograms. Is it likely that someone of Mrs Kruger's stature could deliver a blow with a force strong enough to cause death?'

'Well, she obviously could because her husband is dead.'

'I am not sure if that is an obvious conclusion, sir. Let me rephrase the question. Do you agree with me that Mrs Kruger is a petite, very fragile lady?'

'Yes, she is small.'

'During your examination of the deceased, did you determine his height and weight?'

'Yes, I did. It says so here in my report.' He looked through the report quickly. 'Here we are. He weighed two hundred and fifteen pounds, or ninety-seven and a half kilograms approximately.'

'And his height?'

'He was six feet two inches or one metre ninety centimetres tall.'

'Thank you. Now, my question to you is, given that Mrs Kruger weighs fifty-two kilograms, in your professional opinion, how likely would it be for her to have the strength to hit and kill a man who weighed twice as much?'

Dr Mahere was flustered and the face mopping became more frequent. 'I am not sure how to answer that, Madam.'

'Let me make it clearer. On a scale of one to ten, where ten means very likely, where would you rate Mrs Kruger's ability to kill the deceased with one blow?'

'Maybe between seven and eight. Given that she did succeed.'

'Is it possible that this blow to his head was not the cause of death? Rather, the victim had an old injury which could have been exacerbated by the blow, resulting in his death.'

The prosecutor jumped up to object. 'Your Honour, may I remind the court of the "eggshell skull rule"? This means that the criminal law does not recognise previous injury. Thus, the impact of the lamp is still seen as the principal cause of death.'

The judge agreed. 'Sustained.'

'One last question. During your examination of the deceased, did you determine whether his skull was fractured?'

'Yes, it was.'

'Thank you, Doctor. No further questions.'

The investigating officer was next to give evidence for the prosecution. Sergeant Musekiwa had collected all the evidence at the scene of the crime and had taken witness statements pertaining to the murder and forwarded them to the Office of Public Prosecutions. The public prosecutor then had to decide if there was enough evidence to go ahead with the trial or whether the investigating officer needed to pursue another avenue, person or line of enquiry first.

Since Sophia had already confessed to the crime, the public prosecutor was not required to prove that she had committed the crime; rather, his job was to address the issue of intent. Did the accused intend to kill her husband, or had it been an accident? A domestic squabble that had gone wrong? The officer went through all the events from the time the police were called to the Kruger home on the night that André had died. There were no surprises there; the facts were not in dispute. André went out to drink, came home drunk and the couple began to row, which ended up with him dead.

The prosecutor asked Sergeant Musekiwa to explain the demeanour of the accused when they arrived at the Kruger home.

'She was very calm. When we arrived at the scene of the crime, she was the only one not crying. The daughters and the housekeeper were all upset.'

'Do you think she was glad to be rid of her husband?'

Rudo's annoyance was apparent in her voice. 'Objection, Your Honour. The prosecution is leading the witness. In addition, Sergeant Musekiwa has no way to determine or comment on what Mrs Kruger was thinking.'

'Sustained.'

'Sergeant, was there any evidence to indicate that the accused was remorseful that her actions had resulted in the death of her husband?'

'She was very calm, as I said. She just kept repeating that her husband had been trying to strangle her with his belt, and she hit him on the head with the bedside lamp.'

'So there was no evidence that Mrs Kruger was confused or hysterical?'

'No. Not really.'

'Mrs Kruger says in her statement that she feared for her life, so when the victim bent over to vomit, she picked up the lamp and hit him on his head. Is that correct?'

'Yes.'

'In your opinion, Sergeant, was that the only option open to Mrs Kruger to save herself?'

Rudo jumped up immediately to object. 'Speculation, Your Honour.' The question from my learned friend is leading, asking the witness to speculate on what the Mrs Kruger could have done.'

'Sustained. Would you like to rephrase the question?'

'Sergeant, was there a clear door to leave the room?'

'Yes, there was.'

'What was the distance between where the incident occurred and the exit door of the bedroom?'

'I did not measure it, but my estimation would be around five and a half metres.'

'Was there anything between where the incident occurred and the exit door that would hinder any attempt to leave the room?'

'No.'

'In terms of timing, how long would you estimate it would take to run from where the incident occurred to exit the room?'

'A minute at most.'

'Sergeant, was there any other means of exiting the room?'

'Not exactly, but there is an attached bathroom which is closer to where the incident occurred.'

'No further questions.' With that, the prosecutor sat down.

Rudo stood up to cross-examine. 'Hello, Sergeant. Just a few points of clarification, if I may.'

The officer nodded in agreement.

'In your work, Sir, you have probably been called to many crime scenes where murder has been committed?'

'Not many, but a few.'

'Is it possible that Mrs Kruger was in shock?'

'Of course that is possible.'

'Just to take a step back, Sergeant, you said earlier that there was an exit door about five metres away?'

'Yes.'

'In your investigation, did you determine whether the door of the bedroom where the incident occurred was open, closed, locked or unlocked?'

'No, we did not determine that.'

'Did you see any evidence relating to the fact that Mrs Kruger had been strangled by Mr Kruger?'

'Yes. She had red marks on her throat.'

'Was there any other evidence that she had suffered assault?'

'Yes – her head was bleeding, where her hair had been pulled. Her face was red and swollen, her lip was torn and bleeding, and one eye was swollen.'

'Would you say that these were extensive injuries?'

'Objection, Your Honour. The defence is leading the witness, who is not a medical expert.'

'Sustained. Ms Shava, would you like to rephrase the question?'

'Yes. May I present photographs of Mrs Kruger taken after her arrest as evidence as Exhibit 2?'

The judge agreed. Rudo took some pictures out of her folder and passed them to the court officer. Sergeant Musekiwa was asked to confirm whether the photographs were representative of the injuries sustained by the accused on the night in question. The officer perused them and confirmed that they were.

'Having seen numerous assaults in your line of work and based on your experience, how would you rate the severity of Mrs Kruger's injuries – low, moderate or high?'

'In my opinion, I would say somewhere between moderate and high.'

'So, could you please explain how, while Mrs Kruger was receiving these extensive injuries and trying to save herself, she would have had the luxury of weighing up her options for escape?'

Now the policeman looked confused.

The judge looked at Rudo and asked her to rephrase the question.

'Is it not possible that after being beaten so severely, Mrs Kruger was so confused and afraid that she grabbed the first thing that was closest to her to stop the beatings?'

'Yes, it's possible.'

'I see that Mrs Kruger's statement says that Mr Kruger was using a brown leather belt to strangle her. Where exactly in the room did you recover this belt?'

'We found the belt lying on the bed, near the headboard.'

'Did you take the belt as evidence?'

'Um, yes, we did.'

'However, it has not been entered into evidence as an exhibit.'

The officer was looking uncomfortable. He looked to the prosecutor for guidance, but he offered none. It was the judge who spoke, to seek clarification from the prosecution.

Rudo smiled to herself. This was going to be interesting. The judge, of course, realised that this was an integral part of Sophia's confession. The judge would have to find out why the police/prosecution had failed to disclose, or were withholding, this crucial piece of crime-scene evidence.

'Mr Prosecutor, were you aware of this piece of evidence from the crime scene?'

Again, Rudo was delighted by the oversight. But she kept her delight locked in her heart and along with everyone else looked at the prosecutor gravely.

'Yes, Your Honour, I was.'

'Why then was this piece of evidence not disclosed and admitted into evidence?'

'I will need to determine that, Your Honour.'

'I think that is a good idea,' the judge said, looking annoyed. 'I will adjourn proceedings at this point to allow the prosecution to locate and admit this evidence. Mr Prosecutor, later this afternoon, I will be looking forward to an explanation regarding the omission of this important piece of crime-scene evidence.'

Court was adjourned for afternoon tea. After tea, the investigating officer returned to the stand and presented the old brown leather belt, as directed by the judge. The explanation provided by the prosecutor was that it had been human error on their part. The prosecution had not intended to conceal evidence. If the latter had been the case, he would not have alluded to the belt in his opening remarks, and nor would Sergeant Musekiwa have discussed it so openly. Fortunately for him, the judge accepted this explanation. Court was then adjourned for the day. The next morning, Ambuya would give evidence.

11

HARARE, 2009

The second day of the trial began with the much-anticipated evidence to be provided by Ambuya. Ambuya was more fluent in Shona, her mother tongue, than English, which was the official language of the courts, so the court had provided an interpreter for her.

Ambuya was looking forward to her court appearance and had dressed in her Sunday best. She was a simple, kindly woman who probably did not understand the complexities of courts, lawyers and their skill at manipulating words and laws. As far as she was concerned, she was there to save 'Mama', which is how she referred to Sophia. This was a respectful way of addressing her employer. Even when they were younger than their employees, employers were given the status of parents. As she sat in the witness box opposite Sophia, her eyes remained on Sophia as she answered questions. Sophia did not look up or acknowledge the presence of her housekeeper.

The prosecutor began by asking Ambuya how long she had been employed by the Krugers.

'I began to work there in 1979. This was before Diara was born. There was only Shaan to look after.'

'How did you come to be working for them?'

'I heard that there were new people who had come from South Africa, and they needed someone to help with the housework. Mama, she tell me that they run away from South Africa because the government there did not want *murungus* to love brown or black people.'

Murungus was the Shona word for 'white people'.

'Did they leave South Africa because the police found out they were married?'

'No. Mama told me that she and Baba could not live together, even though they loved each other. The law said they could not marry. Mama lived with her parents. Then they ran away to Zimbabwe to avoid going to jail and so they could live together.'

'Was Baba a good baba?'

Ambuya's response was to look down and rub her hands together in agitation. 'Yes. He loved everyone.'

'What about Mama? Was she a good mama?'

Ambuya smiled at Sophia and nodded vigorously before responding. 'She is a good mama. Always nice to me.'

'Did Baba and Mama behave like they loved each other?'

'Too much.'

'How did they do that?'

Ambuya smiled as she replied. 'They is holding hands and hugging.'

'Then why is Mama saying that Baba used to beat her?'

Rudo objected to this question. 'Objection, Your Honour. You cannot ask a witness why another witness or the accused has said something.'

The judge agreed and asked the prosecutor to rephrase.

'Did Baba ever beat Mama?'

'They were always fighting, those two.' Ambuya managed to evade the question.

'Why did they fight?' the prosecutor persisted.

'Baba would say that Mama did not listen to him. Or she did not cook properly. Sometimes he said that she was liking other men.'

'Objection, Your Honour. Hearsay. The person who purportedly said this is now deceased.'

The judge was silent for a while, looking at his notes. 'I understand you, Ms Shava, but I am going to overrule you on this. It is circumstantial evidence that points to the deceased's state of mind.'

'Did she like other men many times?'

'That is what Baba say – that Mama wanting other men. He was warning her often to not do it, but she was ignoring him all the time.'

'So, Mama and Baba fought when Mama was bad?'

'Objection, Your Honour! That is not a question! My learned friend is drawing conclusions and abrogating the role of the court.' Rudo was annoyed.

'Sustained.'

'Was Baba bad?'

'Only when he was drinking.'

'What bad things would Baba do when he was drinking?'

'Too many things. He broke things in the house. He shouts and swears. Sometimes he is hitting Mama.'

'Did you ever see Baba hit the children?'

'No, no, Baba love them too much.'

Finally, the prosecutor went through the events of the evening on which André had died, asking what Ambuya had witnessed. There were no surprises there.

'Ambuya, did anything different happen that day before Baba went out in the evening?'

'Yes, one thing, and that made Mama angry. Mrs Ndlovu, who lived three houses from us at number twenty-eight, she came to see Mama in the morning.'

'Did she come alone?'

'No. She came with her daughter and granddaughter.'

'Can you tell us what happened?'

'I told Mama that the neighbour wanted to see her and Baba. He was at work. She told me to call them into the kitchen.'

'What did they want?' the prosecutor encouraged Ambuya, who was hesitating and looking at Sophia.

'Mrs Ndlovu, she was saying that her daughter is wife to Baba, and she has a baby by Baba. She is saying Baba is her son-in-law. But he is a bad son-in-law because he has not been to see them for three months and he has not given them money for the baby.'

'What happened after that?'

'Mama, she tell them she knows nothing, and they should speak to Baba.'

'Was Mama angry?'

'Yah, very cross. She told me she was tired of him and his women.'

'Did Mama speak to Baba when he came home from work?'

'Yes, she asked him if it was true that he is daddy to that baby. He was shouting and breaking plates. He try to hit Mama, but she run and lock herself in bathroom. Then I see that Baba go out without eating dinner.'

'The night when Baba died, were you in the main house?'

'No, I was sleeping in my room, which is in the back garden.'

'How did you come to know that Baba had died?'

'Ms Shaan, she come to wake me up. She is crying and crying. She tell me to come because Baba is dead.'

'What happened then?'

'I went back to the house with her. In Mama's room, I saw that she is sitting on the bed with the two younger girls and

Daddy is lying on the floor with too much blood coming from his head. Mama had blood on her nightdress and on her hands. The small girls were screaming and hiding their faces.'

'Did Mama say anything to you?'

'She said that she kill Daddy by mistake, and I should telephone the police. So I did.'

The prosecutor ended his questioning and allowed Rudo to cross-examine Ambuya. Rudo realised that she had to be careful with her questioning, as Ambuya was from a society where men were the breadwinners and the head of the family. The role of the woman was to nurture her husband and children. Thus her views on domestic violence were bound to be of the victim-blaming, perpetrator-absolving school. Rudo was not disappointed.

'Ambuya, did you ever see Mama with other men?'

'No.'

'Did Mama work?'

'No. She stay home.'

'So she could not have met men at work.'

'No.'

'Ambuya, did you see any man come to see Mama when Baba was not home?'

'No. Not me. I did not see, but Baba, he always say it. Baba also tell Joseph to go because Mama was looking at him.'

Rudo looked put out by the last comment. 'Who is Joseph?'

'The boy who works in garden.'

Rudo took the photographs that were taken of Sophia soon after her husband died and showed them to Ambuya. 'Ambuya, these are pictures of Mama on the day that Baba died. Do you remember?'

Ambuya looked at the pictures, then quickly looked away and nodded.

'Why did this happen? Why did Baba beat Mama?'

'He is saying that she not good wife. She does not listen.'

'Was this the first time that Baba beat Mama?'

'No. He do it before.'

The Krugers' housekeeper looked uncomfortable with these direct questions. She glanced at Sophia, who remained impassive and did not lift her eyes from her prayer beads.

'Can you remember how many times he beat her?'

'Many times.'

'How often did he beat her?'

'Every week. Sometimes two times in the week.'

'Has he been beating her ever since you began working for the family?'

'Yes, but it is not his fault. The devil gets in him.'

Rudo was not in the mood to listen to Ambuya's justifications for André Kruger's violence. She knew that evidence from a prosecution witness carried a lot of weight, and she was determined to take full advantage of it. This was the point at which Ambuya could assist her to prove a regular, ongoing cycle of violence. This element was crucial to prove self-defence. She asked the court interpreter to advise Ambuya to only answer the question she was asked. It was time to go in for the kill.

'Ambuya, did Mama ever try to harm Baba?'

'Ah no. Mama is a very soft person. She can't hurt anyone.'

'Ambuya, did Baba beat Mama in front of the children?'

'Yes. Sometimes.'

'Did Mama ever go to the doctor or hospital after these beatings?'

'No. But Baba is buying her headache tablets for pain.'

'Ambuya, did Baba ever say that he would kill Mama?'

Again, Ambuya glanced at Sophia before she responded. 'Yes, he said it.'

'Many times, or just a few times?'

'Many.'

'So, do you think Mama was afraid of Baba?'

'Yes, very afraid.'

'Was Mama afraid that Baba would kill her?'

'Objection, Your Honour!' The prosecutor leapt up, his face a picture of frustration.

'Overruled. I am going to allow it.'

Rudo asked the question again.

'Yes, she was. Very afraid. We were all afraid that he would kill Mama one day.'

Rudo's heart was overwhelmed with joy. She had to make a determined effort not to smile. *Yay! I can show fear and imminent danger,* she thought. Maybe her self-defence argument was becoming a reality. 'Ambuya, you said that Mrs Ndlovu said that Baba was her son-in-law and the father of her grandchild.'

'Yes.'

'How old do you think Mrs Ndlovu's daughter was when she came to see Sophia?'

'Ah, I am not sure. Maybe thirteen years.'

'She was fourteen years old. Your Honour, may I enter into evidence as Exhibit 4 a copy of Tsitsi Ndlovu's birth certificate and the birth certificate of her baby, which lists the father as André Kruger.'

'Noted.'

'Did you know if Baba had other girlfriends or wives?'

'Objection, Your Honour. I don't see the relevance of the victim's love life to our proceedings.'

The judge looked at Rudo questioningly.

'Your Honour, the prosecution suggested Mrs Kruger's infidelity as a reason for marital conflict. This suggestion was based on a third-person account with no substantiated facts. The defence would like to rebut these allegations and explore Mr Kruger's infidelity. Our objective is to provide the court with a balanced picture of the Krugers' marriage.'

'I'll allow it. Overruled.'

'Yes, he did.'

'Did you know any of these other girlfriends?'

'Yes. Some lived in the same road as us.'

'Did Mama know about these other girlfriends?'

'Yes. Some of them.'

'How did she know? Who told her?'

'Sometimes they came to the gate to look for Baba. Another time we went to supermarket and one girlfriend asked Mama for money. She said Baba made her pregnant and now he is cross with her and not give her money anymore.'

'Ambuya, the girls who live on the same road as you – were they as old as me?'

'Ah no, those three are still at school.'

'So it was not the first time that Mama found that Baba had other girlfriends?'

'No. It happened many times. That is what men do. They have many small houses.'

'Last question, Ambuya. Did Baba ever lock Mama out of the house for the night?'

'Yes, but not every day. Only after drinking bad beer at the *shabeen*.'

'How often did he do it? Once a week? Once a month?'

'I think once a month.'

'Thank you. No more questions.' Rudo thanked the witness and sat down, thinking sadly that Ambuya belonged to the generation of women who will look for any excuses to explain men's poor behaviour. Kruger was unfaithful because that's how all men are. He only locked his wife out after he had drunk homemade brew at an unlicensed bar. Again, the brew was responsible for his behaviour, not the man himself. As for her mention of 'small houses' – Rudo seethed inwardly. It was a derogatory term to describe the informal, long-term, secret sexual liaisons of married men.

She had recently found how such secrets, when revealed, can be devastating for the primary wife. Rudo had attended the funeral of a colleague's husband a few months previously. At the graveside, a young woman had appeared with two young boys. They made their way to the area where family were standing. No one thought there was anything untoward, and the wife was lost in her own sad world, having lost her partner of many years. After the burial was over, the young woman approached the wife and began to wail.

'*Amaiguru! Amaiguru!* Our husband has died! Lord help us. Our husband is gone, and we are left alone.' She then pushed her two boys forward, adding that they had lost their father too. *Amaiguru* was the term used to describe the senior wife. Rudo shuddered at the wife's disbelief and utter humiliation that the man she'd thought of as her dear partner had betrayed her in this way.

She was jolted out of her reverie by the prosecution's announcement that they had presented all their witnesses. It was time for the defence to present their witnesses. Rudo stood and called her first witness, who was the private medical examiner she had hired to give an independent statement about Mr Kruger's cause of death.

'Please state your name, occupation and employment history for the court.'

'Dr Davidzo Hatendi. I am a medical practitioner with fifteen years' experience. After I completed my residency at Harare Hospital, I worked for four years at the medical examiner's office. I then returned to work in private practice as a general practitioner. However, I still collaborate with private investigation firms if they require an independent forensic opinion of a death. I am registered with the Health Professions Council as a pathologist.' Dr Hatendi wore his white coat over civilian clothes. He had obviously come directly from his medical practice. He was in his early forties, wore spectacles, and was probably around six feet tall and very slim. Rudo had found he had a very pleasant demeanour, and it did not take much to make him smile. He had a way of talking about deceased persons as if they were still alive, and always referred to them by their first name.

'Dr Hatendi, could you give us an estimate of the number of autopsies you conducted, in your time at the medical examiner's office?'

'I am not sure of the actual number, but on average two to three a week.'

'Have you had an opportunity to examine André Kruger, the victim in this case?'

'Yes, I have.'

'I have a few questions. What was the extent of Mr Kruger's injuries?'

'André unfortunately died from a two-fold injury to his head.'

'What do you mean, two-fold?'

'Well, when I examined his wound, he appeared to have two wounds. First, there was a wound on the back of his head, inflicted by the bedside lamp. Second, André had a massive bruise on his forehead. This was caused by the impact when he fell and hit the floor. I have brought photographs to show the court.'

The clerk distributed copies to the judge and prosecutor, although they had been provided with copies in the evidence file. The picture showed a very large bruise on André's head, about twelve centimetres long and five and half centimetres wide. The measurements were recorded on the photograph.

'Your Honour, please accept this as defence Exhibit 1.'

'Accepted.'

'Dr Hatendi, what was the importance of this wound with respect to Mr Kruger's death, if any?'

'Well, in my opinion, it's an important wound. First, André was hit on the back of the head with a lamp. This caused some damage – there was a skull fracture where the lamp hit him. However, this was a small fracture, as we have all seen. There were blood and bone fragments on the lamp. However, after Sophia hit him on the back of his head, André fell forward and landed on his face. Now I ask you to imagine this big man: he is just ten centimetres short of two metres tall and weighs almost a hundred kilograms. He is very inebriated – literally a dead weight. He fell face down on a hard ceramic floor, having lost the ability to break his fall. The impact of hitting his head with such velocity cannot be ignored. The blood that he was lying in came from his nose, not from the back of his head.'

'So, are you saying that Mr Kruger died from hitting his head on the hard ceramic floor?'

'No. What I am saying is, in my opinion, the trauma to the back of his head and the impact of falling face down on the hard floor together caused his death.'

'Thank you, Doctor. Your witness.'

The prosecutor stood up to cross-examine. 'How certain are you, sir, that your theory on the cause of death is credible?'

'Look, I cannot say with absolute certainty that is what happened, just as I cannot say with absolute certainty that the blow to the back of the head caused the death. I am saying that, in my opinion, it was a combination of both.'

'Dr Hatendi, you receive payment for coming to court to give evidence on behalf of the accused, don't you?'

Before Rudo could object, the doctor did in his own way. 'No, sir, I came here to give a second opinion. We are all paid for doing our jobs.'

Rudo smiled to herself as she noted the prosecutor's annoyed look.

Court adjourned for lunch. Diara would be called by the defence in the afternoon.

12

HARARE, 2009

Diara sat in the small room, waiting to give evidence. She picked up the statement she had prepared for Rudo for use in court and began to read it to refresh her mind. But her mind was blank. Other issues kept intruding. She wondered if Farish was all right. He was with Ambuya somewhere in the court building.

On the table in front of her was a large television. It showed a picture of the main courtroom. The court officials were out to lunch, so the courtroom was empty. The walls of this particular room, where she was waiting, were painted with bright cartoon characters that would appeal to younger children. In the corner of the room, on the floor, was a large cardboard box full of toys. Next to it stood a toy blackboard on wooden legs. To her left were a couple of shelves high up on the wall, on which were male and female dolls representing different skin tones, ranging from dark brown to a cream colour. She recognised them as the anatomically correct dolls that were used to help witnesses to give evidence. Very young witnesses often didn't have the language or comprehension skill to describe sexual acts that had been committed against them. It was often easier for them to show the judge what had been done. The dolls were specially made and had realistic private parts.

Diara knew that most of the people who gave evidence from this room, using closed-circuit television, were children. She knew this because she had been part of a team of donors who had contributed to funding such rooms in courts for vulnerable witnesses. There was one in each town and two each in the two major cities, Harare and Bulawayo, due to the number of cases involving children.

The door behind her opened. She turned to see Sibongile, the court interpreter, come in. She had met her earlier to prepare for giving evidence in this room. Usually, Sibongile would act as the intermediary, so there was no need for direct contact between the court officials, the accused and the witness. This method was deemed to be less traumatic for witnesses, who had already suffered traumatic experiences and now would have to relive them by giving evidence in front of a courtroom full of people – and, usually, the perpetrator.

Rudo had applied through the courts for Diara to give evidence using this system, feeling that this way, the stress on Diara would be reduced.

'Hello, Diara. Are you ready?'

'Hi, Sibo. I'm ready, I think.'

'Don't worry. You will be fine. Just answer the questions clearly. Refer to your statement if you need to.'

At this point, they heard activity coming from the television. People were streaming back into the courtroom. Sibongile sat down at the table next to her. 'I'm right here if you need me. If at any point you feel you need to pause, let me know, and we can ask the judge for a short break.'

There were scrambling noises from the television. The judge had arrived and sat down. All the others followed suit. Diara and Sibo both put on earphones, and Sibo moved the microphone lying on the desk closer to Diara. The camera was focused on the judge, who began the afternoon proceedings by asking Rudo to call her next witness. Diara identified herself as requested and was sworn in.

'Diara, was your father a violent person?'

'Yes.'

'Was he physically violent towards you?'

'Yes, he was violent towards all of us. But he beat my mum all the time.'

'What do you mean by "all the time"? Was it every day? Twice a day?'

'I would say about twice a week on average, mostly at the weekends after he had been drinking.'

'When did this violent behaviour start? Was it recent? In the last five years? Ten years?'

'Longer than that. As far back as I can remember, he has been violent.'

'Can you give us some specific examples of the violent behaviours she endured at the hands of your father?'

'He would beat Mum with his fists or kick her. Once she was down on the ground, he would drag her by the hair and either lock her outside or lock her in the dark shed at the end of the garden, which we used as a storeroom. Usually, Ambuya would wait for him to fall asleep then let her back in. Once, when it was Ambuya's day off, he left her out there all night.'

'How would the violence start?'

'He gave lots of reasons. He said he hated Mum's ugly face, her cooking was bad and cold, and she was a useless wife because she was unable to produce a son. Also, he said she was a "fucking bitch" because he saw her looking at the gardener, and he thought they were having an affair.'

'To your knowledge, did your mother ever report him to the police or anyone else?'

'I doubt it. She was terrified of him. She was not allowed to have friends or to speak to anyone.'

'Diara, was your father violent towards you or your sisters?'

'Yes, but not in the same way.'

Rudo spoke directly to the judge. 'Your Honour, we would like the court's permission for Ms Kruger to read a testimony she has prepared of the violence she suffered at the hands of her father. I believe that this will allow her to relate the incidents in full and minimise trauma to her. Giving evidence of this nature can result in emotional stress as the witness recalls past events. Our legal system allows for this flexibility, so the right of the witness to be heard is not compromised.'

The public prosecutor objected. 'Your Honour, is that not why we are using the victim-friendly court for this testimony? My colleague is now asking for even more leniency on our part.'

'Our legislation allows for evidence to be delivered in this way to minimise trauma to vulnerable witnesses, Mr Prosecutor. I am assuming that the testimony she is going to read is the one that is part of her witness statement, Ms Shava?'

'Yes, Your Honour.'

'Well then, there should be nothing there that you have not already been made aware of, Mr Prosecutor. Objection overruled. I am going to allow it. Ms Kruger is not the accused; she is a witness.'

The prosecutor sat down and Rudo asked Diara to read her testimony.

My father did not use physical violence against my sisters and me; he used other forms of violence against us. It was mostly emotional abuse and sexual abuse. I am going to give you a summary of his violence towards us.

The emotional abuse was usually in the form of statements to demean us or make us feel bad. He would hardly ever call us by our given names. Rather, he referred to us using derogatory names to describe female dogs or female body parts – 'cunt' was one of his favourites. We lived in a state of fear when he was at home. We were always on edge, never knowing when he was going to beat Mum or break things in one of his frequent unmanageable, aggressive moods.

The first time he sexually abused me, I was six years old. This is the first incident that is clear in my mind. I had to stay home from school because I had a cold. Mum was asleep and Dad was in-between jobs. That was usual for him. He had a terrible temper. We had all learned to keep out of his way when we saw signs of it emerging. His temper and aggression also emerged at his workplaces – they often asked him to leave and not come back.

That was a very confusing day for me. I was not quite sure what had happened. Or why. I remember Dad coming into my room. I was dozing from the medicine Mum had given me.

'Are you awake, *skattie*?' he asked. *Skattie* means 'honey' in Afrikaans.

I moaned a response and he sat down on my bed. I was more afraid of his temper than of my symptoms.

'Lie down on your back so that you can breathe better. That's right. You poor thing, your face is burning.' He removed my blanket. 'Let's take this off so that your fever comes down with the cool air.'

He then started to stroke my legs. He started murmuring things that I could not understand or hear.

The leg rubbing was soothing, and my eyes were closing. But they popped open in shock when I felt Dad's fingers creeping into my pants. I held my breath and stared at him, trying to make sense of what was happening. He had his eyes closed, and he was muttering and almost gasping for breath. His breathing was noisy. He started rubbing my private parts. The rubbing got harder and more painful. He gave a last grunt and shuddered. And then he stopped, he opened his eyes and smiled at me, looking dazed and confused.

'You gonna get better soon, *skattie*. Daddies do that to make their little girls better.' He started rubbing my legs again. 'You are getting big, my baby. Daddy must show you these things. Daddy has to make you a woman.'

That episode in my life only became clearer a few months later. Prior to that, I could not find an explanation for it in my six-year-old mind. As time went on, I realised that it had not been a nightmare but reality. From then on he abused both Shaan and me. He took any opportunity to repeat the behaviour that I had experienced. His creativity knew no bounds.

For example, he would pretend that he wanted to help with our schoolwork. He would make me sit on his lap and rub his penis against my vulva, all the while urging me to read louder. We dreaded weekends. He had this routine whereby he would go out drinking at the local *shabeen* and then come home inebriated, shouting and screaming, breaking any objects in his path. I remember my sisters and I would sit in one of our bedrooms, waiting for the inevitable. We would hear the car door bang and then his heavy, unsteady footsteps coming towards the house. The front door would open, then bang shut. Then music would come on. Usually his favourite, 'Bad Moon Rising' by Creedence Clearwater Revival. To this day, hearing that song makes me relive those bad times. It vibrated through the house, bouncing off the walls and increasing our stress levels. Above the music, we would hear him yelling.

'Where the hell are you, woman? Where the hell have you been?'

The music would be turned down.

'How can you hear when the music is so loud, André? What do you want?' That would be Mum's response.

'Nothing from you, bitch. Where are my girls?'

'They are in bed, André. Let's go to bed. Come. Let's go and lie down. It will be better in the morning.'

Then Dad would start beating Mum, then he would drag her across the floor towards the front door while she screamed and protested.

'Get the hell out of here, you stupid bitch.'

He would throw Mum outside then slam the front door and lock it. We would stay in our room, pretending to be asleep, praying that we would not be the one he wanted. He would fling open the door of our room.

'Diara, get into my room. I need a back rub. My back is killing me.'

The 'back rub' would lead to him behaving inappropriately with Shaan or me. He would rub my vulva with his fingers or he would make me lie on him and he would rub his penis against my vulva until he ejaculated.

136

The last time I had to suffer his attentions was so traumatic that I wanted to die. I found all the painkillers I could, and swallowed them. My mother found me the next morning and called an ambulance. At the hospital I was moved to a children's home for further assessment. While at the home, my friend Leanne's parents fostered me. I never returned to my childhood home while my father was alive.

What have been the consequences for me and my sisters of having such a father? I was the lucky one, because my friend Leanne and her parents practically adopted me. They gave me a chance of a normal life. With their support, I was able to finish school, go to university and get a job where I felt I could make a difference.

However, feelings of guilt have followed me everywhere. I feel like a soiled, discarded rag. Incest is not something people get over; it is something they carry with them forever.

Questions always run through my mind when I see children and their mothers. Why didn't Mum protect us from him? The logical, reasonable part of my brain tells me that she had little choice. He almost beat the life out of her. But the angry part of me wants an answer.

The whole time that Diara was speaking, Sophia did not look up, but wept silently. Rudo passed her a tissue. After Diara stopped, Rudo remained seated for a few very long minutes. She drank some water then cleared her throat. 'Thank you, Diara, for sharing your testimony. I just have a few more questions. Are you all right to continue? Would you prefer to have a short break?'

'No. I'm good.'

'How long did your father sexually abuse you?'

'About ten years.'

'Did your mother know it was happening?'

'Yes, I think so. I asked her once when I was about seven if my father did such things to her. And she asked, what things? And I said, "the things he does to my private parts".'

'What was her response?'

'She said yes, it happens to all girls. So I thought it was normal. I hated it and didn't understand what it meant.'

'When did you realise that it was not normal behaviour?'

'I'm not sure. I think slowly, over time. I had to go to the doctor when I was twelve because I had terrible pain when I was passing urine. The doctor had already given me one antibiotic, but it had not helped. The pain came back. So Mum took me back and the doctor said he would take a swab to check which bacteria was causing the problem and prescribe the appropriate antibiotic. When we went back for the results a few days later, the doctor asked to see Mum on her own. I was sitting outside his room, but I could hear them.

'The doctor said, "Mrs Kruger, I am concerned about Diara's test results. The urine sample showed traces of blood and semen. I also noted, when I was taking a swab, that her vulva was inflamed and looked as if it had been rubbed raw. Do you know why that is?"

'Mum said, "No … no, I don't."'

The doctor replied, "There is obviously someone who is interfering with her."

"I don't know who that could be. I will speak to her."

"You need to speak to her – then go to the police. If they need any information from me, I am happy to write a report."

"Thank you, Doctor. I will speak to my husband and get back to you."

'And then he prescribed more antibiotics and told Mum I needed to take them with some water, and we left.'

'That night the shouting and screaming from my parents' bedroom was very loud. I don't know what was said or done but for a few weeks he left us alone. But then he started again. We never went back to that doctor again.'

'After that, did you try to tell anyone else? Ask for help?'

'I asked my friend Leanne what we should do, and we decided to tell our teacher, Mrs Cleary. She kept asking us if we were making it up or whether it was a prank. She then said she would speak to Mum, but I don't know if she ever did.'

'Thank you, Diara. I have no further questions, but I reserve the right to recall the witness should the need arise.'

'Granted. Let us adjourn for the day and begin tomorrow with a cross-examination by the prosecution.'

✿✿✿

Diara sat with Rudo outside the room in which she had given evidence. There was a waiting area for families, and it was also brightly painted with pictures of cartoons. She was drained and exhausted.

'You must be worn out. You've been giving your testimony for over two hours,' Rudo said sympathetically.

'I'm okay. I'm just glad it's over. I've been dreading it for so long that it's actually a relief.'

'Don't be too concerned about the cross-examination. The prosecution will probably try to make you out to be a liar, but you will be able to answer him well. You have truth on your side. Let's meet at eight thirty tomorrow morning. Court is at ten but let's talk a little before we go in. Go over some possible questions.'

'That's fine,' said Diara, standing up to hug Rudo.

'See you tomorrow.' Rudo left with a wave and a smile.

Diara went back into the room and began to gather her bag, files and her statement. Even now, although he was dead, thoughts of her father tormented her. She knew she should feel better – at least feel some relief that her testimony would help to save her mum. But how could she explain to people that it was just the tip of the iceberg? The fear that their father's behaviour had instilled in them was difficult to describe. She could feel old ghosts creeping in at the edge of her consciousness. Ghosts and ghouls whose icy fingers tickled her skin, making her want to scratch herself all over. Ghosts she'd thought she had learned to control or put into a sealed box. The box had now burst open, and the incident she had not spoken of to anyone came ripping out taking her back to her eight-year-old-self.

✿✿✿

Dad is beating Mum again with his fists. She's not moving and there is blood everywhere. I'm crouching behind the curtains with my sisters, praying that she is not dead. We hold our breath, keeping as quiet as we can, waiting ... He finally leaves, with one last kick to her still body. We crawl over to her. I am so scared, lying next to her, holding her hand. I can't breathe. It is wet between my legs. When did Shaan get the wet towel to wipe Mum's face? At last, she moves. I am screaming again because she is not dead. We help her to our room. I must not sleep. If I sleep, she may die. In the morning, mum wakes up, but she is silent, her lips are torn and swollen. I help her around the house, she can't open her eyes. I am terrified to leave her alone in case she dies.

She falls to her knees with no heed to her bag which bursts open with the impact of falling. All the papers fall onto the floor, and without thinking about it, she found herself frantically scribbling it all down on the blank sides of her statement. So desperate was she to get it out of her head and send it somewhere where she could burn it into nothingness.

Oh no! He's throwing all the dinner plates against the wall. Mum is screaming at us. Run! Run away! He grabs Mum by her hair as she tries to follow us, calling her bad words, pulling her to the kitchen. Shaan is screaming for Ambuya. She comes running to the kitchen, sweating and praying aloud. Suddenly Mum's scream becomes a screech. He is sniggering, holding her wrist down on the hot solid plate of the stove. Repeating over and over. 'You like that Bitch?'

Ambuya throws a pot of water on him and the empty pot at his head. She is dragging Mum outside and calling us to follow.

Oh God! Shall I open the door to the trauma of all traumas? The one I have hidden so far down, and not returned to for so long? Never spoken about to anyone, not even to Leanne. Did it actually happen? I throw my pen away. I can't write this down. It will never go away.

Dad comes home. Angry and drunk. As usual. Mum is answering the telephone. He comes up behind her and kicks her on her bottom. The phone drops. She turns, only to be kicked in her swollen tummy where Ambuya says she is growing a baby. 'You bitch! You made me lose my job!' He is shouting after her as she runs to her bedroom. He follows and we hear a thud. Creeping to their bedroom door. Mum is crouching on the floor, screaming, begging him to stop. He is kicking her with a crazed look on his face. Over and over. We are crying. Oh no! He's seen us. We freeze. Swallow our cries. He freezes. We run back to our room, creep under the covers shivering and fearful. Shaan and I clutch each

141

*other. Heavy footsteps are coming towards our door. The
front door bangs and we breathe again. Mum is lying curled
on the floor, sobbing softly. We lay down with her and try
to stroke her to comfort. She tries to hug us but ends up
screaming clutching her middle*

*'Mummy! Mummy!' Shaan is howling. 'Go fetch
Ambuya. Both of you. Go now.'*

*She is screaming again, shrieking with pain. Then I notice
the big patch of blood on the front of her skirt. I am so,
so scared. I can't leave her in case she dies. Shaan is running
to fetch Ambuya. I sit near Mum, stroking her and asking
God to help her.*

Perspiration drips off her brow. Diara rocks, her eyes
closed, in a self-soothing mechanism that she has used since
childhood. Simultaneously, she sings in a monotone:

'Thula thula thula baba. Hush, hush-a-bye baby.'
'Thula thula thula sana. Hush, hush-a-bye baby.'

Her favourite bedtime song, sung by her mum in Zulu.
She opens her eyes. They are unfocused. Her rocking
continues. She shakes her head and allows herself to recall
the incident, thumping the table she is leaning against with
her fist. Trying to refocus. Tries to sing louder, but her chest
is tight. She has begun to wheeze.

*Ambuya gently turns Mum onto her back, the blood
has spread across her dress and is dark. We gasp with
horror and fear. Ambuya runs to the bathroom, comes
back with towels. Why are we not lifting Mum onto the
bed? Why is Ambuya laying towels and a pillow under
Mum? Is she making Mum comfortable to die? Mum is
groaning with pain. Tears are pouring down her face.
Ambuya is bending Mum's legs at the knees before she
realises, we are still in the room.*

'Go to your room girls and shut the door.'

Mum is screaming again. We scurry out, terrified. Sit on our bed, listening. We lie down and wait ... I wake up abruptly. Mum's screams are even louder, interspersed with words of comfort and encouragement from Ambuya.

'Shh ... *zvakanaka* ... it's all right. Shh, Mama, it's okay.'

I wake Shaan, and we run back to Mum's room and stand at the entrance looking in. They are in the same position as when we left, on the floor, but Mum is lying with her head on a pillow, on top of old towels. Ambuya is still kneeling between her legs, shaking her head and looking miserable. She is holding something. A bloody, slimy doll. The size of a large carrot.

We watch in confused silence as she wraps the little thing in a towel and holds it out to Mum, who is looking away, gasping loudly, as if she has been running.

'*Myweh*, Mama. It's a boy! Ah, God is testing us. It's a boy!'

Ambuya is wailing, trying to shove the little parcel into Mum's arms. Mum is keeping her arms firmly wrapped around herself, her eyes tightly closed. Tears are running down her cheeks. Ambuya sighs and lays the little bloody parcel down. Helps Mum to the bathroom. The sound of the shower filters through. I walk slowly towards the mysterious bundle lying on the floor. Shaan hangs back. It's a little doll, but a dirty one. I lean down and touch its tiny cheek. Warm and wet. Just then, Ambuya opens the bathroom door. I run back to Shaan; we go back to hide under the covers.

'What's happened, Dee? What's happened to Mum? I'm scared,' *she says through her sobs.*

I have no answers. We are woken by thumping and banging on the front door. Shaan screams, and I feel her nails pushing into my back through my cotton pyjamas. The front door opens.

'Do not come in, Baba, you have done a bad thing. You are a devil.'

'Get out of my way, you stupid bitch!'

'No, Baba! Stay outside! You have killed your son, and Mama nearly so. Here, say sorry to this little thing that you forced out of its mother. His spirit is still here. He is cursing you for what you did to his mother.'

'What have you done, you bitch? What is this?'

There is an eerie silence, followed by an almost dog-like howl.

'You fucking bitches! What have you done? Let me in! Sophia! You killed my boy! I am going to kill you all!'

'Get out, Baba! Get out! I will call the police. Mama is bleeding too much. I will show them the marks from your beatings. Get out, you devil! Sit outside and listen to the spirit of your son cursing you.'

The door bangs and we hear the key turn. Ambuya makes her way back to Mum's room and closes the door behind her. There is no sound from outside. The next morning, we are standing near our bedroom window, which overlooks the front garden. Dad is under the jacaranda tree near the wall, digging a hole with a shovel. On the ground is the small bundle. He digs a shallow hole, throws the bundle in and covers it up.

'You must forget this. Never talk about it to anyone.'

Ambuya comes into the room. She puts her finger to her lips, made a shushing sound and leaves the room. We never went near that jacaranda tree again, afraid of the evil spirit living there.

'Show me how to forget all this Ambuya?'

In Diara's testimony, she did not mention many specific incidents. She and Mandida, in discussion with Rudo, had decided that it was not a good strategy to list every single violent memory, but rather for her to present information in a reasonable fashion in a way that would be digestible to the court. Too much detail could work against them. They could be accused of exaggeration – especially as they had no corroboration. Their mother had not reported the abuse to anyone, had never involved the authorities.

Diara sat rocking and crying silent tears.

'Hi, Diara.'

She looked up at the sound of the familiar voice and was shocked into silence. 'Xander!' She felt her eyes welling. *Oh God. I am so pathetic. I can't believe he is here. How? What?* She ran across to him with little regard for her belongings, which flew onto the floor. She threw herself at him, and the force of it made him stagger back against a table behind him. He held her, hugging her tightly. The familiar smell of him was so comforting that, try as she might, she could not contain her sobbing. He said nothing, just stroked her hair and hugged her tight with his other arm. Diara was agitated, despite his attempts to soothe her. She would tap him on the chest with her fist, or pull his hair, all the while sobbing. Finally, he forced her to look at him.

'Dee, tell me what to do. How can I help?'

Diara took some deep breaths and tried to regain some semblance of control. Xander looked devastated. He had found a tissue from somewhere and was gently and slowly wiping her face, while wiping away his own tears. She felt shattered.

'What are you doing here?' she asked. 'How did you know I was here?'

'Leanne called and said that you were in Zim for the trial. She was worried because she couldn't get away to be with you.'

145

'I know. She was upset about that, and Aidan is away on one of his stories. It's all a bit crazy now.' She knew she was talking for the sake of talking, trying to regain her equilibrium after her traumatic day.

He waited for her to finish. 'I wish you had told me, Diara.'

'I know. I just didn't want to worry you by telling you the trial date. You have so much going on …'

'I was in the courtroom when you were giving evidence.'

'Oh …' She turned away and went quiet. Xander put his hands on her shoulders but did not speak. All Diara wanted to do was throw herself on the floor and weep. She could not bear the fact that he knew all that sordid stuff about her. She felt dirty.

After an interminably long time, she took a deep breath. 'It's hard. I wanted to tell you that night in Jo'burg, but I chickened out. Can you imagine telling your friends stuff like that? That's the last thing I ever wanted you to know about me. I thought it would change how you thought of me.' She stopped so she could wipe her nose and think for a minute. 'The thing is, I have learned over the years that no good comes from telling anyone these stories. Most times, they're not sure what to do with the information. Somewhere along the way, you realise that so many others have a similar story to tell and your story is just another story. I remember I always wanted to have regular parents, like everyone else at school. I envied children whose dads picked them up from school. It just seemed so normal. If my dad had come to fetch me from school, I would have run a mile.' Diara took a deep breath. 'But really, what is normal? We all assume that being normal means having a fabulous life with no trauma. But most people have some awful stuff in their life – and that's what's normal. We all carry baggage of some sort. Everyone is living with pain. Most people have suffered some trauma. The best way to deal with issues is to tell someone, talk to someone ... but then what? We still have to wake up the next morning and get on with our lives. No one can do that for us. So I stopped looking for outside help. I refused to let my bad experiences define me. I tried to own them. I tried so hard to move on, looked for my own inner strength or whatever it's called, and vowed to always protect myself from being hurt again. It's so much easier to be a victim and blame everyone else.'

She stopped and covered her face, overcome by emotion. Xander patted her shoulders and upper arms soothingly as she leant against him. Finally she turned around, wiping her face. 'But whatever I do to move on, that bastard won't let me. On days like this, I feel like I am running, running as fast as I can because something hideous is chasing me. Only to find that it's me. I am hideous.' Diara emphasised her last words by jabbing herself in her chest. Tears were rolling down her cheeks again. Every breath she took crackled and rasped. 'You just don't know, Xander. You don't know how it feels. It's a horrible, horrible sensation – it's like death, but no one dies. I'm still alive. Hideous me is still alive.'

Xander found another tissue to wipe her face. He pushed her hair back from her face, ran his hand down it and wound it around his hand to hold her steady and keep her close. He rested his chin on the top of her head. Slowly, the stiffness eased from her body and she relaxed against him. Only then did he say anything.

'The only thing it has done is give me a better understanding of you. I can only admire how you have managed to survive after facing all that ...' He grappled for words. 'But look at you – you've made an amazing life despite everything that happened to you.'

Diara had started to cry again silently. He held her tighter and continued to stroke her back. Eventually, she pulled away and looked up at him, a lot more composed. Her face was red and her eyes were red and swollen. Her eyeliner was smudged around her eyes, giving her the look of a wounded animal. Diara moved away from Xander and scrabbled in her bag for another tissue to wipe her face and eyes. The room was silent. Finally, she felt collected enough to turn around and face him. Xander also looked overcome with emotion.

'I decided that the best thing I could do was to get on. Even if he had been arrested or had his testicles cut off or whatever, I still had to live my life. I didn't want what he did to us to be the most important thing in my life. I wanted to have a life that was so far removed from him that I would never be reminded of him.' As she spoke, in the back of her mind she felt an intrusive nudge of fear. She realised that she had to get away from Xander ... or else more complications were going to arise.

'What time is your flight back?' she asked abruptly, taking Xander by surprise.

'I can take either the early morning flight or the evening one tomorrow. Or I can stay longer. I want you to tell me what you need. I'm happy to stay if you need me to. I'm staying at the Brontë.' He named a lovely boutique hotel in the suburbs which had beautiful meeting rooms named after the Brontë sisters.

'Okay. Let me check in at home with the girls and freshen up. I probably look like Alice Cooper,' she said nervously. 'I'll come up to the hotel. We can have a late dinner and talk some more.'

'That's fine, but let me take you home. I hired a car at the airport.'

Diara was panicking. She started to pick her things up off the floor, trying to reassure him and persuade him to leave. 'No, don't worry. Shaan will fetch me. She must be on her way. You go on – I'll see you later.'

Instead of reassuring him, he looked confused by the abrupt change in her behaviour.

'But I want to wait with you. It's not like I have anything else to do.'

When she did not respond, he asked her again, 'What's wrong? You're being weird.'

'Nothing's wrong. I just don't want you to wait around getting bored while I'm sorting myself out.'

'Dee, stop that,' he said, holding her shoulders. 'I want to help you sort your stuff out.'

Just as he was speaking, the door opened. Ambuya stood there with a disgruntled Farish. 'Sorry, Missy Dee. Baby is hungry.'

Diara and Xander stopped talking. Diara froze. Xander looked bemused. He looked at the baby, then back at Diara, as if seeking clarification. She did not give him any. She could not bring herself to meet his eyes, which were frozen accusingly on her. Quickly, she walked over and took the boy from Ambuya, putting him over her shoulder and soothing him with comforting noises.

'It's all right, Ambuya, thanks. Why don't you go outside and wait for Shaan, then go on home with her? I will come home with my friend.'

Ambuya looked at Xander and smiled a greeting. She put the baby's nappy bag on the table and left to meet Shaan. Diara, perhaps motivated by guilt or by being faced with this unexpected scenario, didn't know what to do. She sat down and unbuttoned her blouse to feed the baby, making soothing sounds and speaking quietly to him. It was only after Farish had settled down on her breast that she dared look at Xander. Their eyes met as he lifted his from the sight of the baby feeding, and he stated the obvious in a shocked tone.

'You had a baby.'

'Yes. I had a baby.'

'I don't understand. Why didn't you tell me? Am I so unimportant to you?'

She was unsure how to respond and was still grappling with what to say when he added, 'Is that why you avoided me when I was in London in the summer?'

She nodded.

'I suppose Leanne wasn't allowed to tell me either?'

She nodded again.

Diara looked at Farish, who was kicking and fidgeting. She took him off her breast and held him over one shoulder as she hooked up her feeding bra. She rubbed his back, kissed him and stroked his hair, all the time aware of Xander's eyes on them. She offered Farish her other breast, still stroking his hair. Taking deep breaths, her heartbeat settled and calmness flowed over her. During the feed, Xander remained silent, watching her. She realised that she had to talk: if she continued to keep him in the dark, there would be no coming back from that. He would never forgive her. His reaction told her he believed that she had run off and had a baby with another man, some nameless, faceless entity.

'Xan ...'

'Diara ...'

They spoke at once. Xander held up his hand. Then the penny dropped; she did not have to tell him. He had done the sums.

'Dee, I want to ask you something and I want you to tell me yes or no. Please. If you value us, don't lie to me.'

She looked at him and nodded. 'I'm so sorry, Xander. So, so sorry. I feel so, so bad.' She realised that her babbling was falling on deaf ears. He looked devastated. He slumped in his chair and covered his face with his hands. She waited for him to say something. After what felt like an eternity, he looked at her, his expression angry.

'What the fuck, Diara? Didn't you think that I had a right to know? Aren't you tired of living with secrets?'

The injustice of his remark stung. She kept her anger in check as best she could, speaking in a normal tone so as not to frighten Farish. 'Do you not think I wanted to? Every day since I found out, I have wanted to tell you. But you didn't sign up for this. Do you think I wanted your wife to find out that I was pregnant when she was struggling to have a baby? I didn't want to hurt her like that. If I hadn't come to see you for my own selfish reasons, this would never have happened. I took advantage of you.'

Xander gave a sarcastic laugh. 'Are you crazy, Diara? I was a willing – very willing – participant.'

She stared at him, not sure what to say next. Luckily, Farish spat out her nipple and wriggled to sit up. He gurgled, chewing his fingers and staring at the stranger, who stared back. She held him against her hip as she tried to hook up her feeding bra and button her blouse.

'Here, give him to me.'

Xander took the baby, who continued to stare at him curiously. Diara finished dressing and picked up her belongings. Mentally drained, she realised that there was nothing else to say. Xander needed time now.

'We had better go. They will be locking up the building soon. Are you still all right to drop us home?'

'Of course.' He stared at her incredulously. 'Why would I not be?'

They did not speak again till they were in the car, driving to Diara's home. She sat in the back with the baby. Xander drove in silence after he asked her for the address. Diara took a deep breath and began talking. The silence was killing her. 'I want to explain a little more, Xander, but please, you have to stop being angry.'

He said nothing. Just stared straight ahead.

'When I found out I was pregnant, I was so, so confused. I told Leanne and she urged me to tell you. I was so mortified that it had happened. I didn't want you to feel like I had planned everything. All I wanted was to see you and tell you how much you meant to me. I finally felt I could, now that *he* was dead. I had waited for years to get close to you at varsity, but I failed. I didn't have the courage. Then courage grew out of the corpse of a monster. Big mistake. The monster got the last laugh. Stupid me. Did I really think I could grab happiness and get away with it?'

She stopped and took a deep breath. She felt that she was ranting, and her chest felt tight. She blew her nose and wiped her face before continuing. Xander remained silent as he negotiated the rush hour traffic.

'I tried to have an abortion. I even went to the clinic.' Again, she stopped. Did he care about any of this? It was hard to tell. He just stared straight ahead.

'But I couldn't bring myself to have the abortion. I could not bear to add another layer of trauma to my life by killing our baby. At any other time, I would have welcomed this new life because I had made it with you. But now ... having a termination would have been easier all round. Then when I went for my first scan, I was told that I might not carry the baby to full term – I have scarring and damage to my cervix, most likely from him, from what he did to me and the sexually transmitted disease that resulted. So, when I really wanted to tell you, when I wanted you to be there and share all these precious moments with me, I told myself, why bother? I would lose the baby anyway. So I came up with excuses not to tell you.'

Diara paused. She needed to explain all the reasoning behind her decision. 'There was also my stupid pride. I couldn't bear for you to take me on for the baby's sake. I knew you wouldn't abandon me. I felt like an incubator. And now that you know about Farish, your life will become much more complicated.'

She looked at him in the rear-view mirror as she explained. Farish had dozed off with the soothing motion of the car. Xander continued to stare at the road ahead.

She hesitated, feeling embarrassed and not quite sure how to describe it. 'But I know I was wrong. When all is said and done, I was wrong not to tell you.'

This time he did look at her. 'Yes, you were.'

There was nothing more to say. They remained silent for the remainder of the drive. When they arrived at her home, Xander got out of the car and took the baby from her so she could gather her bags and papers. She handed them to Ambuya, who had opened the gate for them. Xander was holding the sleeping baby in the crook of his arm, stroking his hair. 'He's incredibly beautiful,' he said solemnly, looking at her.

Dee just nodded. She didn't trust herself to speak. 'Leanne says he looks like you, but he has my hair and mouth.' Moving closer, she continued, 'He even has a dimple in his chin like you.'

There was silence as they stared at the sleeping baby.

'Why don't you come in for a while? Let's talk some more. Please.'

'No. I don't want to do that, Dee. I think I'll just go to the hotel.'

'Okay. I understand.' She was disappointed and her heart felt sore. She felt limp and raw. Her body ached – she felt as if everything had been sucked out of her. She wanted him to stay. She wanted to talk about everything that had happened today, but she knew she had hurt him. She had made him feel idiotic. Powerless.

She took Farish from him and leant against him briefly. 'I'm so sorry, Xander. I have hurt you, but I thought I was saving you pain.'

'I know,' he said, 'but in fact finding out like this was infinitely more painful. If I hadn't come here to see you, would you ever have told me?' With that he got in his car and drove off, not waiting for an answer. She walked to the front door, wondering if she would ever see him again. She went inside. It was going to be a long, restless night for her.

13

HARARE, 2009

The next morning, Diara heard a car horn as she was getting ready to go to court. Shaan came into her room and surprised her by saying, 'Dee, Alexander is here to see you. Who is he?' She asked the last question in a whisper.

'Oh, okay. Will you take Farish for a bit? I'll just finish getting dressed. I've just fed him and bathed him.'

'I can't, Dee. I have to leave now if I'm going to get to work on time. Ambuya's in her room getting ready for court.'

'Of course. Sorry. Give him to Xander, please.'

'But … won't the baby feel strange?'

'No, Shaan, it's fine. He will be all right with him.'

As Shaan opened her mouth to ask more questions. Diara held up her hand. She felt bone weary. 'Let's talk about that later. Let me just get through today, okay?'

Shaan reluctantly picked up Farish from where he was playing on the bed and left. Diara finished dressing and hurried out. *Another day in paradise*, she thought. Xander was sitting with Farish on his lap, blowing on the baby's face. Every time he blew, the little boy cackled and wriggled with delight. Then he would close his eyes and wait for the next gust of wind. Diara stood some distance away and enjoyed watching them.

Xander looked up and saw her. 'Hi. I thought you might need help with the baby while you're in court.'

She nodded and smiled weakly. Her heart felt happy. She should have realised that Xander would not abandon her to the wolves. He did not smile back, just turned his attention to the baby.

Their silent drive to the court was broken only by Farish's babbling and Ambuya's responses. On arrival, they made their way to the witness waiting room to meet Rudo. The two younger women embraced.

'Rudo, I'm not sure if you remember my and Leanne's friend from varsity, Xander Joubert.'

'He looks familiar,' said Rudo, smiling. 'Rudo Shava. Glad you came. Diara really needed support. And this little guy too.'

Xander took Farish from Diara and said to Rudo, 'I'll take the baby so you two can talk.'

'No, it's fine, Xan. Please stay. I'm going to have to feed him before I go back to court.'

'I'm just outside. Call me when you're done.'

Diara watched him leave.

'Well, well, Diara Kruger! You are a dark horse. I wouldn't mind a piece of that.'

Diara smiled.

'And he's good with the baby.'

'Yes, he is.'

✪✪✪

Diara returned to the vulnerable witness room and spent the morning being questioned by the prosecutor. This reaffirmed her reasons for never talking about her childhood. As soon as she did, people's perception of her changed. Although the prosecutor was just doing his job, it was humiliating to have to justify herself in the face of the wrongs that her father had committed against her. Rudo had warned her that the prosecution would ask unreasonable and sexually fueled questions to destabilise her emotionally in court. She had been urged to remain calm and non reactive.

'Ms Kruger, yesterday you said in your testimony that your father carried out a number of sexual acts against you and your sister from the time you were six years old. Is that correct?'

'Yes.'

'How often did it happen? Please give us an estimate.'

'Once or twice a week. Sometimes less. Sometimes more. It depended how annoyed he was with life and how often he went drinking.'

'So you can remember clearly from the age of six that he committed these acts against you?'

'Yes. I remember that it was a very fearful part of our lives. We grew up with the fear always there in the background.'

'In this abuse that allegedly occurred, you described a variety in your testimony. Did he supposedly subject you to all of it every time?'

'I'm not sure what you mean.'

'I mean, the variety of sexual behaviours that you said your father conducted with you. Were they the same ones every time or did he perform several on the same night?'

Rudo jumped up angrily. 'Objection, Your Honour. Relevance. What does the variety – or not – of the sexual acts matter? The law does not regard underage children as willing participants in any sexual activities. This line of questioning is irrelevant and is likely to exacerbate secondary trauma for the witness.'

'What is your point, Mr Prosecutor?' the judge asked.

'Your Honour, I am trying to establish the credibility of this witness.'

'Well then, do so, but pursue a different line of questioning.'

'Yes, Your Honour. Ms Kruger, could you summarise for the court the sexual acts your father carried out against you?'

Diara tried hard to stay calm. She was not going to allow this man to blame her for the abuse or make her feel as if she had been an active participant. She took a deep breath and responded as if she were describing a visit to a supermarket.

'He progressed from less intrusive to very intrusive sexual acts. In the beginning, he would rub my vulva with his fingers, but he would not look at me while he was doing it. He would lay me on the bed on my side and lie behind me. Sometimes he would sit me on his lap. The first time he exposed himself to me, he blindfolded me and placed my hand on his private parts, his hand covering mine, urging me to rub harder and harder. Once he got used to the idea of exposing himself, he would do it more often. Does that answer your question?'

The prosecutor looked taken back by her clinical response. He had obviously been hoping to draw a reaction from her. However, he recovered very quickly. 'You stated earlier, Ms Kruger, that both you and your older sister were subject to abuse?'

'Yes.'

'Is it possible that there was more of a relationship between you and your father than you are admitting?'

'I don't understand.'

'I put it to you that you enjoyed the attention your father showered you with. You had formed an unhealthy attachment to him, and your alleged suicide attempt was because his attention had strayed to your sister and others in the neighbourhood.'

'Objection! Your Honour! I object strongly. That is not

a question, but an inflammatory statement to elicit a response from the witness. Where is the information to support the statement and what on earth does it have to do with the case?'

Rudo took a deep breath to calm her nerves. The audacity of the man!

'I also object because the law is clear. Ms Kruger was legally unable to agree to such behaviour. She was a child. My learned friend's statement is not only insensitive and devoid of factual support, but it is also objectionable.'

'Mr Prosecutor, I agree with the defence counsel. All her objections are sustained. Sir, I would strongly advise you to abandon this approach to questioning.'

'I apologise, Your Honour,' he said, looking anything but apologetic. 'Did you have a toxic relationship with your father? Were you envious of any other women in his life?'

With difficulty, Diara maintained her deadpan expression and responded in a monotone. 'First, I was not a woman when these incidents occurred. I was a powerless, confused little girl. My motivation was not to remove all my "competitors"; it was to get as far away from my father as I could. I succeeded in doing this. I left home at fifteen and the next time I saw him he was a corpse.' Diara felt she had responded well. Rudo was trying to hide a smile, and the prosecutor was pretending to peruse his notes.

'How many people did you talk to about the alleged abuse?'

'I tried to talk to my mother about it, but she didn't want to listen. She said that he was a mad person, and we should just avoid him.'

'Did you tell anyone else? The police? Another family member?'

'When I was fifteen, I told Dr Kaputa, the psychologist at the hospital.'

'So, after nine years you told a psychologist?'

'Yes.'

'You allowed your father to continue abusing you for nine years before you told anyone who was in a position to assist you?'

'I did not *allow* him to abuse me. He forced me. I was a child. What could I have done?'

'So, Ms Kruger, we only have your word that this abuse was actually happening for all those years?'

Rudo stood up. 'Your Honour, asked and answered. Ms Kruger has already given testimony to significant persons who knew the abuse was going on.'

'Sustained. Ask a different question, please.'

'Ms Kruger, are you married?'

'No.'

'Do you have a significant other?'

'No.'

'Any children?'

'Yes. A son.'

'Do you know who the father of your child is?'

'Yes.'

'Are you in a relationship with the father of your son?'

'Yes, we are friends.'

'Objection, Your Honour,' Rudo said. 'What relevance do these questions have to the case at hand?'

'Your Honour, we are highlighting Ms Kruger's deficits as a character witness. She is a single mother with no significant relationship. I would question the quality of her evidence.'

Rudo was furious. 'Are you saying that because she is a single mother, she is a liar? If you are a single mother, you are automatically a liar? According to the 2007 United Nations Report on the Status of Women in Zimbabwe, almost fifty per cent of households are headed by women. Are they all liars too?'

'What are you saying, Mr Prosecutor?' the judge asked directly.

The prosecutor seemed to realise that he had gone too far. 'Withdrawn, Your Honour. Ms Kruger, you love your mother very much?'

'Yes.'

'It must be difficult for you having her in jail.'

'Yes.'

'Would you like to save her from any further jail time?'

'Yes.'

'Even if it means exaggerating or embellishing what actually happened?'

'I did not have to do that.' Diara was losing patience. She had to breathe deeply and try to remain calm. Rudo had told her not to react to the prosecution's tactic of deliberately provoking her. Much to her relief, the prosecutor, after asking a few questions to clarify her testimony, ran out of questions and Diara was excused. The judge called a break for lunch. Diara found Xander with a fast-asleep baby and Ambuya in the witness waiting room. He stood up as she came in, looking questioningly at her.

'It was okay. Not so bad,' she said.

'Let me go and get us something to eat,' said Xander, moving towards the door.

Diara made to follow him. 'Let me come with you.'

'Why don't you stay here? The baby will probably need a feed,' he said, not stopping to give her the option.

Diara sighed and realised that he was still not ready to talk to her.

❁❁❁

The afternoon sitting began with Rudo calling Mandida as her next witness.

'Raise your right hand and repeat after me,' the clerk of court requested.

'I swear to tell the truth, the whole truth and nothing but the truth. So, help me God.'

'Duly sworn in, Your Honour,' the clerk said to the judge. 'Please state your name and occupation for the record.'

'Dr Mandida Kaputa. I am a clinical psychologist, registered with the Health Professions Council. I am employed by the University of Zimbabwe School of Medicine to teach behavioural sciences to medical students.'

'How long have you worked for the medical school?'

'About fifteen years.'

'Dr Kaputa, do you also see individual clients admitted to the hospital who may need psychological intervention?'

'Yes. I do that on a regular basis at the hospital, and for follow-up at my weekly outpatients' clinic.'

'Please tell us how and under what circumstances you met my client, Sophia Kruger.'

'I actually met her second daughter, Diara, first. She was hospitalised at the age of fifteen as she had overdosed on painkillers. The doctors attending such a case in casualty must refer the patient for psychological support and intervention.'

'Is this when you met Sophia?'

'No. I telephoned Mrs Kruger repeatedly to ask her and her husband to come in to discuss Diara, but she kept putting it off, claiming ill-health.'

'When did you finally meet Mrs Kruger?'

'I discussed the case with the medical social worker at the time, Kudzai Khumalo, and we decided to do a home visit.'

'So you actually met Mrs Kruger at her home on Anzac Road in Meyrick Park?'

'Yes. That was the one and only time.'

'Could you please give us a summary of your meeting with the Krugers?'

'When we arrived at the house, Mrs Kruger would not see us. She claimed to have a migraine. While we were at the house, Mr Kruger – the deceased – arrived home from work. Mrs Kruger only emerged from her room when Mr Kruger yelled for her to come out.'

'What were your impressions of Mr Kruger?'

'He was aggressive and suspicious of us. He also tried to minimise Diara's attempt on her life. He described her as "stupid and ungrateful". I asked him why Diara didn't want to come home. He said that he didn't know but that she was, and I quote, "hoity-toity and thinks she's too good for us".'

'And Mrs Kruger? What did she have to say?'

'We only met her for a few minutes – she promised to come in the next day. She was timid and obviously fearful of Mr Kruger. As were the two younger children – they shut themselves in their bedroom as soon as they realised Mr Kruger was at the gate.'

'Objection. Your Honour, the witness is drawing conclusions about the accused. Speculation. As is the reason the two younger children shut themselves in the bedroom.'

'Sustained.'

'Did Mr and Mrs Kruger come in to see you about their daughter?'

'No.'

'So they never bothered to come in and discuss their daughter's issues with you?'

'No.'

'Could you tell the court what happened with Diara after she left the hospital?'

'Well, she refused to go home. Kudzai Khumalo, the social worker at the hospital, and I were battling to find a way forward with the case. So, as an interim measure, with Diara's permission we moved her, once she was physically stronger, to the children's home in Eastlea. We wanted to place her in a neutral environment and evaluate her progress. Psychologically, she was still very fragile, given to bouts of weeping and long silences. We also wanted her to be in an environment where we could visit her regularly. We did not feel that Mr Kruger would welcome us in the family home.'

'Over this period, as you met with Diara did you get a clearer picture of what was troubling her?'

'Yes.'

'Could you share it with the court?'

'Yes. Very briefly, and only because Diara has given me permission, to do so.'

'We understand that you have a legal obligation of confidentiality to your client. However, these confidentiality obligations do not apply if the information you have reveals a criminal act. So please rest assured that you are not breaking the law.'

'Diara disclosed that Mr Kruger was hurting them.'

'Hurting who?'

'Her mother, Diara and Shaan, the eldest daughter. Mrs Kruger was a victim of domestic violence, both physical and emotional. Her husband beat her on a regular basis, almost weekly. And she was constantly belittled and criticised by him.'

'And the girls?'

'He was sexually abusing them. He had been over a long period. In fact, according to Diara, since she was around six years old.'

'Dr Kaputa, could you give us some idea of what forms this sexual abuse took?'

164

'According to Diara, he began by making one of the girls sit on his lap and rub him until he ejaculated. Or he would use his fingers to rub their vulva and penetrate their vagina with his fingers while he masturbated.'

'Was the abuse limited to the behaviours that you have described?'

'As far as I gathered from Diara, and as is common in situations such as these, the sexual behaviours progressed to him rubbing his penis against her vulva and ejaculating on her.'

'So is that why Diara took an overdose?'

'Partly. My understanding was, the night before she took the overdose, Mr Kruger got carried away and penetrated Diara's vagina with his penis. She screamed and tried to get away, but he held her down. That was the trigger for her taking the tablets. Now she was afraid of consequences, such as pregnancy and sexually transmitted diseases.'

'Dr Kaputa, are you not required to report this kind of situation to the police?'

'Yes. We wanted to, but Diara was adamant that she would not give a statement to the police. She said that if they arrested her father, her family would be in financial trouble since he was their only source of income. In addition, he always threatened to kill their mother if the girls told anyone anything about their life at home. Diara worried constantly about this threat. Believe me, this is the biggest regret of my life. If I had reported him, perhaps we could have saved the other girls from being abused by him.'

Mandy went on to describe how Diara had stayed at the children's home for almost a year before Leanne's parents applied to foster her and she went to stay with them. She also explained Leanne's relationship to Diara.

'Did the Krugers ever visit Diara at the home?'

'Not the father. Mrs Kruger came a few times with the girls, but it was difficult for them because she could not drive. They saw each other more when Diara was with the McKenzies, Leanne's parents, because the two homes are only about a kilometre apart.'

'Dr Kaputa, did you have any further contact with the victim, Mr Kruger?'

'Only once. It was during Diara's first year at university. She came to see me because Mr Kruger had taken to driving to her hall of residence and waiting for her in the car park. It was usually at the weekend, after he had been drinking. He would beg her to come home as "he missed her and loved her so much". I am quoting what Diara told me. She did not know what to do, as she didn't want to involve the police.'

'What did you suggest?'

'I told her to leave it with me. I went to see Mr Kruger at work. I told him that we had written a report about his sexual violence and that if he continued to harass Diara, I would have him arrested for rape, stalking and harassment.'

'Is that not against the law?' Rudo asked with a small smile.

'I don't know. You would know better. We were making the best of a toxic situation. After that, he did not come near Diara again.'

'Dr Kaputa, what are some of the consequences of this abuse on Diara?'

'Two weeks after Diara left home, we found that she had a sexually transmitted disease, chlamydia. She was brought back to the clinic from the children's home as she had a high temperature, vaginal discharge, pain in her stomach and lower back, and it was very painful for her to pass urine.'

'Are you sure that the source of the infection was her father?'

'Well, not in absolute terms but on a balance of probabilities, I would say that yes, he was the source.'

'Is it possible that she contracted it from a boyfriend?'

'In my opinion, that's highly unlikely. When I met Diara she was suffering from post-traumatic stress disorder. This is a disorder that is usually suffered by soldiers returning from war and conflict. It is also common in children and women who have suffered conflict in an intimate situation. A person she should have been able to trust took advantage of Diara repeatedly. Diara suffered night terrors and intrusive thoughts for many years. In other words, no matter what she was doing, suddenly her thoughts would be invaded by her traumas. As Diara put it: "Mandy, whatever I do, having coffee with Leanne, looking at dresses in shops, smiling at a boy, that bastard is always there. He's always there, reminding me that he screwed me." So no, I don't think she had the emotional strength to go out and look for a boy to have sex with.'

'In your opinion, how often do children lie about being sexually abused? Is it not unusual that she took so long to report these alleged incidents?'

'I've not met any children who have lied to me about being sexually abused. Diara did try to tell her mother, her teacher, her doctor – but they all failed her. Our system failed to protect her. Diara was different from most of my cases in that she disliked her father. She had lived in a home full of violence and trauma. She did not feel guilty about reporting her father. But she feared for her family's safety. Most children, when they are sexually abused by their father, cannot make sense of it. They carry terrible feelings of guilt because they cannot say no to the father they love.'

Rudo thanked Mandy for her testimony and the prosecutor stood to begin his cross-examination.

'Dr Kaputa, we have heard testimony from Ms Kruger and yourself that she suffered sexual abuse at the hands of her father – the victim in this case.'

'Yes.'

'Did you at any point try to corroborate this allegation? For example, when you first met Ms Kruger in hospital, did you examine her using a rape kit?'

'No, because by the time Diara told us what had happened, too many days had passed to get any meaningful forensics.'

'So, apart from the fact that she developed this infection, there is no evidence that her father was the source of the infection?'

'No.'

'So, no corroboration.'

'Not from a rape kit. No.'

✿✿✿

'How was Mandy's testimony?' Diara asked Xander. She was in the witness room with the baby while he had been in the court.

'She did very well. There was not much the prosecution could refute.' Xander hesitated, then added, 'You had a tough time with your parents. I learned how tough today.'

'I know, but I can't cry about it. I can't allow myself that luxury.'

'You held your own in the cross-examination, though. Some of those questions were ridiculous!'

'Yes, but they always are in these cases. I've sat through various cases in this court. Some of the questions asked were so ludicrous, you wonder how intelligent, educated people can't see how absurd they sound.' Diara took a breath and looked off into the distance, realising that she was becoming agitated again. After a few minutes she spoke again in a monotone, which she usually did when she was trying not to be emotionally overwhelmed. 'Unfortunately, it happens all the time. As soon as you are raped or abused, you are the last thing that is considered. The abuser is the one with all the power. My mother told us to keep quiet because our father was our family's only source of income. My father told us he would kill my mother if we told anyone. And if a case makes it to court, then the legal system has problems too. It's not unheard of for magistrates to excuse abusers by claiming that the child looked older than she was, so the perpetrator made a mistake that anyone could have made. Or children are generally liars, so we can't take their word for anything.'

She took another deep breath and gave a shaky laugh. 'I rationalise all this by accepting that this is how people cope with the subject of abusing children. They have to find an explanation that's palatable to them so they can cope with the information. It's easier to believe that the child is a liar than to admit that your husband loves having sex with children.'

Diara waited for Xander to say something. She felt a compulsive need to talk – as a way of expressing her pain, perhaps? She wasn't sure. She just couldn't stop. It felt important for Xander to understand everything about her life. 'And you know how people have this stereotype of paedophiles as weirdos, crazy people? They couldn't be more ordinary. When you look at a group of them and try to come up with reasons for why they behave as they do, it's scary how normal they look to the outside world. They're usually heterosexual, married, with children of their own, and like football and drinking beer. Just like any other guy. I guess that's why it's so difficult for people to believe accusations against such men. They're so ordinary.'

She realised she was babbling. Babbling so he would not say what he really wanted to.

'People are misinformed,' he responded.

She looked away, wishing they could talk about something else. Xander sat down opposite her. 'I'm going to catch the early evening flight back to Jo'burg.'

Silence followed.

'You're still angry,' Diara said, resignation in her voice. 'I'm so sorry that I hurt you. It was not my intention. I was being selfish when I came to see you. I wanted to be in a normal relationship and didn't think about all the consequences.'

'No. No. I'm not angry,' he said, reaching across the table to take her hand. 'I stopped being angry ten minutes after I left you last night. I shouldn't be angry. We have a beautiful baby.'

She kept a brave face as she responded. 'Please don't worry. I'm not expecting you to change your life in any way. Don't do that for me. If you want to see the baby, come whenever you want.'

'Thank you. I would like to. I also want to send you money every month for him.'

'No ... that's not necessary. I manage.'

'I want to. Please let me.'

'Xander, taking money from you doesn't feel right. But I understand that you want to, so I will send you the details of the savings account I set up for Farish and you can send money to that. It will be useful for him when he's older.'

He nodded. 'I'm going to leave for the airport in an hour – let me take you home. I have checked out already.'

She sighed and nodded. What was left to say? Nothing much. All had been said – and done. He had chosen his route. He wanted to see his son and he wanted to send money for his upkeep. Exactly how she had predicted it would go. *Are you watching this, Leanne?* she thought.

Farish finished feeding, then started to struggle, wanting to go to Xander. He came over and took Farish. Diara gathered all their paraphernalia and they left for the car park. The drive home was quiet, with only the baby making noises and throwing his toys around. But it was not uncomfortable, as the last one had been. Xander took Farish from her when they arrived home. He was sleepy as Xander kissed his head and put him down in the stroller Diara had fetched from inside.

'I'm going to go straight to the airport. I have to return the car as well.'

'Thank you for coming,' she said. 'It was so good of you.' They embraced and, during the embrace, she said, 'I will never ever be sorry I had him.'

'Me neither,' he said, to her surprise. She lifted her head and looked at him.

'Dee …'

'No, it's fine. Please go. This is very painful for us.'

'I was going to say that I will do the best I can for you both.'

Diara looked up at him and stroked his cheek down to the cleft in his chin. He looked down at her and rubbed his thumb against her bottom lip. A kiss that began as a gentle goodbye became so much more. She clung to him, sobbing, and he tried to comfort her. She felt so wretched. So helpless.

'I know you will, Xan.' She stepped back and he turned to go. He paused and turned back, and she quickly wiped away the ever-ready tears.

'Here's the thing, Diara. So often, I close my eyes and I can smell the apples in your hair, see how you look when I touch you. The soft sighs. I can feel your hands on my back and your hair all around me. I've never felt like that before. But I'm finding it hard to accept what happened – that you got pregnant and had our son alone.'

His anger was escalating, and so was her sobbing. She felt cruel and selfish, on top of the feelings of terror, anger and self-hate the trial had brought up. She ran back to him and tried to cover his mouth to stop his words. 'Please help me, Xander, I can't cope. Don't turn on me. Take me back to my new happy place where you are kissing me and touching me and it's not dirty and shameful. Take me to that place where you have no wife.'

When he heard this plea, his anger deflated immediately. He pulled her close. Now there were only her sobs and his soothing sounds. After a while he spoke again. The gentle Xander was back. 'I'm so sorry. I'm a shit.'

'Xander Joubert, you are doing me in. Go away before I lock you up and never let you go!'

'No. Your problem is, you can't believe that anyone can care for you.' He hugged her tightly, kissed her temple and left. It took all her strength and willpower not to run after him and beg him to stay.

As he drove off, she couldn't help wondering if he would tell his wife about the baby. She felt a great deal of discomfort at the thought.

14

XANDER AND SASKIA, JOHANNESBURG, 2009

Xander jumped into his hire car and drove quickly away from Diara. It had been a strange and immensely powerful day, emotionally. In fact, he had no words to describe the emotions he had experienced over the past two days. There were a myriad of them. The overwhelming one was terrible, terrible guilt. He had single-handedly brought chaos into the lives of three people. One of them was too tiny to realise how his life would be affected. Xander was conflicted. He didn't know how he could make everything right so that he felt comfortable. He realised that he had to tell his wife about the baby and his relationship with Diara. Hang on – was it a relationship? He slapped the steering wheel in frustration. Was it frustration? He wasn't sure. He felt physically sick and his thoughts were jumbled. He couldn't concentrate on anything for more than a few seconds.

Could he get away with not telling Saskia about the baby? People did it all the time. Lived a double life. They lived, hoping and praying that their two worlds would never collide. But he knew that he didn't want Farish to be an ugly secret while he continued to live with Saskia and pretend the baby didn't exist. He didn't want to live a double life. He could not disrespect either Saskia or Diara in that way.

He was distracted momentarily as he went through the process of returning the car and checking in for his flight home. Not in a thousand years would he have guessed that his trip to Zimbabwe would end this way. He had arrived yesterday morning really looking forward to seeing Diara. He had hoped they could talk about what had happened between them in Johannesburg after her father's funeral. Why he had wanted to talk about it again was not clear to him. She was obviously not interested in any further discussion. She had asked for nothing from him and had since returned to her former demeanour towards him. Distant and polite. That was how she had always been towards him, ever since they had met. Not just to him, though; she was like that with everyone except Leanne. Leanne! He pulled out his mobile and texted her. He checked his watch and noted it was six o' clock in the evening in London, so she was bound to be home.

Were you ever going to tell me?

Her response came fifteen minutes later as he was boarding the plane.

It was not my secret to tell. But I did try to tell you in my own way. Sorry, Xander. Xx

He sighed, shut his eyes and leant back in his chair. She was right. It wasn't her secret and she had put her friendship with Diara at risk by asking him to go to Zimbabwe. He really couldn't blame her.

He thought back to when she had called him at work four days earlier.

'Xander, I need you to do something for me.'

'Sure. What's up?'

'Look, I know it's short notice, but do you think you could nip up to Harare for a few days?'

Xander had given a yelp of disbelief. 'Okay. I wasn't expecting that!'

'I know, and I'm really sorry to ask. Aidan is away and my classes have exams, so there's no way I can get away. Dee's mother's trial starts in two days. I'm really concerned that she's battling through it on her own.'

Xander was quiet as his mind clicked through the practicalities of taking time off work, on one level, and seeing Diara, on another level. He found that he could not think of any great obstacles.

'Xander? Are you there?'

'Yes. Yes. Sorry, I was just thinking about the practical issues about work and taking time off. I think I can manage to do that for a few days.'

'Wonderful. That has really put my mind at rest. I can't bear for her to be on her own.'

Now it was clear to Xander that Leanne had had more than the trial on her mind when she had sent him there to support Diara. She had probably disagreed with Diara's decision to keep the baby a secret. But he knew that he could not compete with the strong bond the two women shared. My God! A baby! His mind was reeling. In one second, his former stresses had been replaced by new ones. But he had to admit that, deep down in the recesses of his mind not governed by the rules of conventionality, he felt a strange pleasure at being a father. But he had never in all his years imagined that Diara would be the mother of his child. Not the Diara he had known for years. Despite all the time they had spent together in a group, *that* Diara had been an unknown entity. Along for the ride but revealing little of herself.

Xander recalled the first time they had met. He had been intrigued by her physical appearance. She was an incredibly good mix of her mother's Malaysian heritage and her father's white Dutch background. Although she favoured her mother more, he had realised in court yesterday, when he had seen Mrs Kruger for the first time. Diara had her mother's light caramel-coloured skin, tawny eyes and delicate frame, and probably her dark hair, which was hidden by a headscarf. However, while her mother's face was round, Diara's was oval, with high cheekbones. This, along with her thick, dark hair – which reached halfway down her back – and her daily uniform of jeans, shapeless shirts and canvas shoes, made an unusual combination. It was almost as if she was unaware of how attractive she was, or didn't want to draw attention to it. Well, it all made sense now. Her emotional distance. The fact that she'd never had a boyfriend in all the time he had known her. He should have realised on the night Farish was conceived that he was her one and only relationship so far. She had practically told him so.

He often thought back to that evening. In the beginning, he had justified it to himself as two friends, struggling with life, finding comfort with each other. However, as time went on, he realised that thoughts of her were intruding more frequently than before. He had been looking forward to seeing her last summer. He had thought they could talk more about that night and come to some kind of understanding about it. And – if he was honest with himself – he had just wanted to see her again. When that hadn't happened, he had brushed aside his disappointment and moved on. She didn't feel the same and didn't want to see him.

Saskia. He rubbed his face to erase her image, but it would not leave. She was almost a stranger now. A mostly silent wife with a brittle laugh. Often, he would look up and she would be staring at him, hostility in her eyes, which she would quickly try to disguise. He spent a lot of time alone – she was often at her parents' house in Cape Town, probably escaping from him. Whenever he brought up a topic such as adoption or fostering, she either went to Cape Town or locked herself in her room till the next day. He wanted to distract her from her pain and offer her a way to move on. She saw it as him sprinkling salt in her wounds.

She had become more silent as the weeks passed, and his attempts at conversation or suggestions of joint activities together were not well received. She stayed in their room for days, lying on the bed, staring at the wall. Work, friends and her other usual activities were forgotten. He had left her alone for a few days, but panic set in when the days passed and became nearly two weeks. When she told him that she could see her babies playing in the corner of the room, he had contacted their family doctor to visit her.

The doctor had diagnosed her with post-partum depression. He was concerned that the depression would progress to psychosis, since she was delusional and thought that the babies were in the room with her. He had suggested a short period of hospitalisation to help Saskia to recover, along with a psychiatric assessment and perhaps medication. Saskia had resisted this suggestion and become hysterical, insisting that she could not leave her babies. Finally, the doctor was forced to tranquillise her and call an ambulance. It was five weeks before Saskia came home from hospital. The resident psychiatrist had prescribed antidepressants, which took two weeks to stabilise her mood. After this, she attended a hospital support group for women who had suffered the loss of a child. By the time she came home, her mental health had improved. She went back to work and attempted to go back to her life as it had been before the loss of their babies. However, her psychologist felt that Saskia's progress was hindered because she had unresolved issues with her husband, and suggested couples counselling for them. Xander had seen this as an opportunity to discuss their issues with a mediator and map a way forward. How could it not be useful? But it turned out to be a little more complicated.

Saskia had accumulated enough 'evidence' in her mind to blame her miscarriages on Xander. This 'evidence' included his long working hours, which had meant he wasn't supportive enough after she miscarried the first time. So, because of this, she miscarried the second time. Apparently, she could 'see blame in his eyes whenever he looked at her'. She told their counsellor that 'she couldn't bear to look at him because she felt like a failure'. Xander could handle this. He felt that she needed reassurance to help her get over these feelings.

What he hadn't realised was that these issues were just the tip of the iceberg. In the fourth session, Saskia had confessed that she'd had a fling with Cecil – Xander's friend from university. Cecil, the commitment-phobe, the one who was always eager to share details of his numerous one-night stands. Apparently, according to Saskia, Xander's coldness and lack of support had driven her to look for comfort with Cecil.

Maybe she was right. Maybe he hadn't supported her enough after the miscarriages. He thought he had. And now the baby with Diara? That would break them. He did not think that their marriage could survive his telling her about Farish. But he knew he had to.

❁❁❁

Xander drove up the drive leading to his home in the suburb of Dainfern. Theirs was one of twelve homes in a gated community. The entrance to the estate was manned by guards in a bulletproof shelter, with entrance and exit gates to either side. He pressed his remote to open the gate. Only visitors reported to the guards. As he drove up to number eight, he realised that there was no way he could soften the pain for his wife. He felt terrible. He knew he was going to hurt her. But there was no other option. He had to tell her. There was no way he was going to hide Farish. That wasn't fair to the child. Or to Diara. No matter how much she blamed herself for that night, he carried equal blame. He could have left. He was married. He sat in the car, lost in thought for a long while before he found the courage to go in and face his wife.

Saskia was sitting at the dining room with her usual glass of wine. She was still in her work clothes. She worked in the public relations department of a pharmaceutical company. As usual, she was impeccably groomed. Her straight blonde hair was cut in a stylish bob. The style enhanced her cheekbones and gave her a gamine look. Her green eyes were magnified by immaculate make-up. Saskia refused to go out without make-up. At the beginning of their relationship, Xander had found that strange. Her skin was smooth and clear and, to him, she always appeared more approachable and vulnerable without make-up. But even after her miscarriages, she never went out without make-up.

She smiled and looked up as he came into the room. 'Hi. How was your trip?'

'It was good. How are you? How was work today?'

'Exhausting. How is Diara? How is the trial going? Is it over already?'

'No, no, not yet. I think it's going well. But you can't tell with these things.' Xander hesitated. How would he bring up the issue of the baby? He felt sick. But there was no way out of it. 'Sas, there's something we need to talk about.'

She looked at him questioningly. 'Is everything all right?'

He had her attention now and there was no going back. 'Sas ... Diara has a baby. A boy. His name is Farish.'

'Really? Well, I wasn't expecting you to say that.' She looked confused.

Xander was still thinking about how to share the next, and more important, part of the story, when Saskia said, 'I didn't know that she was pregnant. Did Leanne tell us last summer? I didn't even know that she was seeing anyone. Did you?'

'No, she didn't,' he responded to the first half of her query.

'Very strange girls, those friends of yours.'

She stared at him. 'Oh God, Alexander, this isn't one of your schemes to adopt a baby, is it? I can't deal with that now. And I certainly would not be interested in Diara's baby. He will just be as strange as his mother.' As she spoke, she poured herself more wine.

Xander took the plunge. 'No, it's not a scheme to adopt a baby. I don't have to. He is my son too.'

There was silence.

Xander waited for her reaction, feeling even worse. Like a sneaky, cheap adulterer.

She continued to stare at him in silence. It disconcerted him.

'I did not know about the baby till I got to Zim.'

More staring.

'I'm sorry, Sas. I ... we did not plan on this happening.'

Saskia began to cry.

Xander continued nervously. 'It know this will be a shock, but maybe we can talk ...' He knew he sounded ridiculous, but he was at a loss for words.

She leapt up and threw her glass of wine onto the floor. The glass smashed and the wine spread quickly. Her face was flushed, and beads of perspiration stood out on her lip. Her face was full of horror. More tears flowed, and she brushed them away angrily. 'What exactly did you want to talk about?' she said, her voice cold and composed. 'The fact that you fucked someone else? Or the fact that I'm a complete failure as a wife? Look how easy it was for that bitch to have a baby. How long have you been fucking her? Now it all makes sense. Now I understand why she's always been so cold to me. She wanted you for herself, the poisonous bitch!'

Xander's shame grew. He did not respond. The depth of Saskia's anger was apparent in her use of words that she normally would not say. He wasn't sure whether to say any more.

Saskia turned on her heel and left the room. He heard her in their bedroom, drawers opening and closing, then after a few minutes the front door banged. She did not come home that night. Nor would she answer her mobile when he called her repeatedly. After his tenth call, she messaged him to say she was fine and not to call her again.

The next day when he got home after work, the house was in darkness. Her things were gone from their room and she had left a note for him saying that she was driving to her parents in Cape Town and would he please give her some space to think. That was the last time he heard from her directly.

15

SOPHIA KRUGER

The last witness Rudo called to the stand to speak on behalf of Sophia was the psychologist who had assessed her and submitted a report. The evaluation had been Plan B for the defence. Rudo had indicated early on to Diara that it might not be a good idea to put her mother on the stand. Rudo knew that Sophia found reasons to excuse or justify her husband's behaviour.

'Your Honour, the last witness I would like to call is Dr Inviolata Marimo. She is an expert in domestic violence and its consequences for victims. Dr Marimo has spent more than eleven hours with Mrs Kruger over a period of eleven weeks and has prepared a report of her findings. We have submitted the report as an exhibit for the consideration of the court.'

'Yes, I have read the report,' the judge replied. 'Mr Prosecutor, do you have a copy of the report? Good. Then let us take thirty minutes to refresh our minds as to its contents.'

PSYCHOLOGICAL ASSESSMENT
Name of Client: Sophia Kruger
Date of birth: 16 January 1964
Age: 45

Terms of reference for assessment

1. To obtain a full background and history of client.
2. To assess the mental health status of the client.
3. To ascertain the extent of violence perpetrated against the client, if any.
4. To offer a psychological opinion as to whether the client could premeditate and plan a murder.

Childhood and early history

Sophia is the eldest of three children. She has a sister and brother who are two and three years younger than her, respectively. According to her, her family are practising Muslims and have a strong faith. Her parents and siblings still reside in Cape Town, where she was born and where she lived until the age of fourteen. She has not been in touch with her family since she left Cape Town.

Sophia describes her ethnic origin as Cape Malay. Her ancestors were brought to South Africa by the Dutch East India Company in the 1600s as slaves, and they in turn introduced Islam to South Africa. The Cape Malay cultural identity includes people from South and Southeast Asia, Madagascar and local Africans.

Sophia describes her parents as extremely strict Muslims. Her father is a religious cleric known as an imam. As a result, her parents set rules for their children relating to friendships, clothing, prayer and dietary requirements, as dictated by the tenets of the faith. Sophia has worn a headscarf from the age of five, in line with Islamic tenets advocating for modest dress for males and females. This was a demand made by her father, and she has worn the scarf to this day.

She told me that she was never allowed to leave her home without it, or she would be punished or beaten by her father.

Her father, Imam Abrahams, served at one of the local mosques in Bo-Kaap, a neighbourhood near the city centre, which has historically always been a Cape Malay quarter. Sophia attended Claremont Moslem School, which is where she met her husband, the victim André Kruger (DOB 15 May 1951). She was fourteen years old.

André was part of a construction crew that was building a new block of classrooms parallel to Sophia's form room. This was the room in which Sophia often spent free time. She described herself as a shy child. André would often look through the window of her classroom and smile or wave at her. At first, she did not pay much attention, but after a while she started to look forward to seeing him every day. She began to open the window and talk to him. He would sometimes leave little treats for her on the windowsill – a sweet, a chocolate or an apple. One day she told him about three boys who often waited for her after school and pulled off her scarf or tripped her up. That day after school, when the boys were trying the same stunt, André appeared from nowhere and saved her, reprimanding the boys. It never happened again. Sophia soon became overly attached to him. In her own words: 'I could not believe that such a man, a white man, would want to see me again and look after me. It seemed like a miracle. How blessed was I?'

At this stage, Sophia perceived her meetings with André as 'very romantic'. They started to meet in the workmen's shed, which was more private and secluded.

From now on the information she provided is sketchy. She jumps to relate how, on one of these meetings, he 'made her his wife'. She gave no other details. I assumed that she meant that André had sex with her. The next detail she provided was that she felt sick for a week after this, and vomited often. She became so weak that her mother took her to the doctor. The doctor confirmed that she was pregnant. Her father beat her until she admitted who was responsible for her pregnancy. Her father went to find him. She does not know what transpired between them, but two days later André came to their house. Apparently, he told her father that he wanted to embrace Islam and marry Sophia. Her parents were very unhappy about the marriage but gave in after being counselled by the head Imam in charge of the local mosque. Sophia said that her parents were more concerned about the neighbours knowing that she was pregnant than they were about her.

For the first month of their marriage, Sophia lived with her parents and André lived at his flat. They could not live together due to the prevailing legislation in South Africa, which forbade marriage between white people and those of a different race. After a month, André asked her father to arrange a passport for Sophia, as he had decided that they should move to Zimbabwe (then Rhodesia), where they could live together. So, after eleven weeks of marriage, they made their way separately to Bulawayo, a city near the border. Her father accompanied Sophia on the bus. In Bulawayo, a friend of her father arranged for them to be driven to Salisbury (now Harare) and stay with a family until they found their own accommodation.

Violence against Sophia Kruger

Sophia was very reluctant to discuss her husband's violence. She often praised him for being a 'loving, hardworking man who would do anything for his family'. Sophia speaks of him as if he is present and not dead. It was apparent from our discussions that she has no friends and has no contact with any outsiders, except the housekeeper and gardener. It was only in our ninth session that she provided any information about her husband's violence, and this was only after I showed her the photographs taken by the medical examiner in her file. At this stage, it became apparent that she was still in denial about her husband's violent tendencies. The depth of her denial is demonstrated further by her tendency to refer to her husband in the present, as if he is still around. She believes that she was not a good wife to André, and the following are some of her beliefs about her inadequacies as a wife. I quote:

You see, Doctor, I was married young. I did not finish school and I did not know how to cook the food that André likes. I am also not particularly good at keeping house. André has extremely high standards and if we do something in the house that displeases him, he gets angry. I have disappointed him in many ways. I have been unable to give him a son. We have four girls. The one time I was pregnant with a boy, we lost him. I blame myself for this because I made him angry. He kicked me in the stomach, and his kicks took away my little boy.

Sophia talks about her husband as if theirs is a great love story. Again, I quote:

André is such a loving man. He wants me all to himself. I think it hurts his heart if I talk to any other man, even the gardener. Also, he says I am not good in bed. You see, the problem is that I often have migraines. When I do, it is difficult for me to be interested in him or even to smile.

Her denial of her husband's violence made it difficult to establish how often he was violent, and to find out more about actual incidents. However, Sophia shows other classic signs which lead me to believe that she is a battered woman. First, she told me that she tried to avoid any situations that could result in his anger and violence. This phenomenon is called 'walking on eggshells'. For example, she made sure that the curtains were all closed before he got home, the way he liked them to be. He had been known to pull them down if he was not obeyed. In addition, she mentioned that she never refused to have marital relations with him, as this angered him. Her interpretation of this is that it was his overwhelming love for her that had made him angry. She does not see that she had the right to refuse or delay marital relations for any reason, such as feeling unwell.

Second, Sophia spoke frequently about how André had suffered in his childhood. Once, when inebriated, he had told her about a great love he had had – a relationship that no one had approved of. It was apparently taken away from him, and he had never recovered from the loss. This phenomenon is referred to as the abuser displaying a 'vulnerable side'. A battered woman will use this as evidence for hope that the relationship will improve or come right. Further hope comes from incidents of 'small tenderness'.

For instance, in the curtain example above, if André was not abusive on one occasion, even though the curtains were left open, the victim used this as proof that her partner was not all bad and there was hope that things would improve.

Third, when Sophia was asked why she did not leave the abusive situation, her response was, and I quote, 'Why would I do that? I love him. Allah will reunite us in heaven. I often dream that he is waiting for me in a beautiful field.'

Violence against the children

Sophia did not want to discuss her husband's violence towards her daughters. In the final session with her before compiling this report, I questioned her about the written testimony provided by Diara to Mrs Kruger's lawyer. I asked Sophia directly if she was aware that Diara had said her father had been sexually abusing her for almost a decade. Her response was that Diara had a history of fabricating stories and she was a 'traitor' to the family. She went on to say that Diara had made up the abuse so that she could leave home and live with her friend Leanne.

Denial is a psychologically incapacitating mechanism used by a victim to screen out distressing realities. In my opinion, Sophia is in denial about the sexual abuse her daughters suffered, just as she is in denial about why her husband physically abused her. She blames herself for all the physical abuse she suffered at her husband's hands. In my opinion, a mother's denial of the abuse can be even more damaging than the abuse itself. It is even worse when the mother reacts to disclosure with anger and punishment. Having said that, the denial is understandable: Sophia, along with other women in similar situations, lacks the emotional and psychological resources to deal with sexual abuse and domestic violence.

Conclusions

In conclusion, I did not find any evidence that Sophia Kruger has mental health issues that may have led to her having murderous tendencies. Her state of denial about the violence she and her daughters experienced in their home is a defence mechanism. Sophia has been presented with facts that she finds too uncomfortable to accept. So she rejects them, insisting that there is no truth in them, despite what looks like overwhelming evidence. Denial is a coping mechanism that provides an individual with time – time to adjust to traumatic situations – for example, the loss of a loved one. Sophia's denial has become harmful. It has had devastating long-term consequences for herself and her daughters. This behaviour is common in women who have suffered many years of physical violence. Violence, for Sophia, has become normalised – a normal part of life, something to be expected. She came from a childhood home where physical violence was used as a form of punishment, and went to a marriage that had similar dynamics.

So, did Sophia plan to kill her husband, or was it an accident? In my opinion, which is based on my decade of experience at the domestic violence shelter and my interviews with the client, I am confident in saying that it was an unfortunate accident. Sophia is still in denial that her husband was a violent man who controlled her with violence. She lived with the illusion that he exhibited enormous love for her. Since he had also suffered during his childhood, she was confident that his vulnerable side would one day surface and he would miraculously realise the error of his ways and they would live happily ever after.

Sophia is not unusual in this response. A large majority of women who are physically and emotionally abused do not stop loving their partners – in fact, all they want is for the abuse to stop. So, they hope. I saw no evidence that Sophia had, during her marriage, ever planned to leave her husband. I believe the idea never occurred to her.

After half an hour, the judge asked if everyone had reread the report. Satisfied with the responses, he gestured to Rudo to continue.

Rudo stood up. 'Dr Marimo, thank you for your assessment of the accused. I have a few questions for you. How would you describe the behaviours that André Kruger used to woo Sophia while she was at school? Would you describe it as normal courtship?'

'Well, since at the time Sophia was fourteen, and a minor, and Mr Kruger was twenty-seven, I would describe his behaviours as grooming his victim, with a view to having sex with her. Which is exactly what happened: Sophia was pregnant at the age of fourteen.'

'Yes – after what is legally termed statutory rape, since Sophia was too young to consent to sex. Dr Marimo, why do you feel so strongly that the accused had no plan to kill her husband on that night?'

'On that night, like many other nights in her life, the accused was just trying to save herself from her husband's violent assault. He was much stronger than she was, and his strength was enhanced by alcohol. Despite all the violence she had endured, Sophia never once spoke about plans to leave her husband. When I asked her why she had not left him, her response was "Why would I do that? I love him." I believe that she had accepted this as her lot in life, and she would probably have gone on living with him.'

'Thank you, Dr Marimo. Your witness.'

The prosecutor stood to cross-examine the expert witness. 'Dr Marimo, is it possible that, on the night in question, Mrs Kruger killed Mr Kruger in an emotional, angry reaction to his alleged ongoing infidelities and abuse?'

'It's possible but not probable in this case, and it was not the first time Sophia had had to deal with her husband's infidelity.'

'Exactly. Her husband was apparently physically abusive and had affairs. As her hurt and anger accumulated and as his defences were impaired by alcohol, she saw this as the perfect opportunity to get rid of him once and for all.'

'Objection, Your Honour. Is there a question here? Or is the prosecutor giving us a sermon?'

Before the judge could rule, the prosecutor backed down. 'Withdrawn. You indicated in your report that Mrs Kruger denied her husband was abusing her daughter. Could Diara, as a child, have made these allegations up to manipulate her parents?'

'It is very unlikely. Perhaps I need to explain the concept further. Women who are victims of violence often adopt a psychologically protective mechanism of denying the existence of the abuse or incest or both. This allows them to continue their lives without facing the painful reality that they hate their husband for beating them. Acknowledging this truth may end in the breakdown of their marriage. Sophia was facing a mind-splitting dilemma: the man who groomed her and had sex with her when she was fourteen was doing the same to her daughters. She found it difficult to reconcile the fact that her husband, who she states "loved her so much" and was so perfect, in her mind, was committing a moral atrocity against her daughters. In other words, the mechanisms she uses to cope with her own abuse are the same ones she uses to cope with the abuse of her daughters.'

'If you believe in Diara's incest claim, Doctor, is it possible that Mrs Kruger was jealous that her husband was having sex with her daughter?'

Although Dr Marimo looked shocked at the question, she managed to respond. 'It is possible, but highly unlikely.'

'Doctor, is it possible that this fight was between a mother and daughter over Mr Kruger, and it ended in the death of Mr Kruger? Perhaps they were tired of sharing his attentions?'

Rudo leapt to her feet, incensed. 'Objection, Your Honour, this question has no basis in fact. There is no evidence to support Mr Prosecutor's suggestion of collusion between Mrs Kruger and Diara related to Mr Kruger's death. Furthermore, may I remind the court that Diara was in London when Mr Kruger died?'

'Sustained.'

For the first time, the psychologist addressed the judge directly. 'Perhaps I have failed to provide an adequate explanation for the court about the Kruger family. The prosecutor's last few questions give me the impression that he suspects that the women in this family fought over Mr Kruger. This was not the case. The violence and incest in the Kruger family were psychologically traumatic for all the women involved. These episodes are difficult for survivors to put behind them: they stay with them, no matter what help they receive. Some individuals just cope better than others. So, describing this psychologically damaged family as mother and daughters fighting over a man is disrespectful and an attempt to normalise the abuse and incest that took place. Sexual abuse of minors leads to significant trauma; we cannot marginalise it or attempt to minimise its significance in this trial. Nothing excuses someone from raping children. Nothing. Research shows that men like Mr Kruger, who are physically and sexually violent, behave in this way to control women and children. He saw them as possessions to use and abuse as he saw fit. He did not see them as people.'

16

HARARE, 2009

'Your Honour, this is a remarkably simple case to sum up. Sophia Kruger, the accused, has confessed to killing her husband, André Kruger. We have all accepted that as the truth. My question is, was it really an accidental death? Let us examine the events of that day and perhaps we will be able to draw some conclusions.

'Mrs Kruger's morning was interrupted by a visit from a neighbour. The neighbour had her young daughter with her, and her granddaughter. Mrs Ndlovu, the neighbour, had come looking for André because he had failed to visit his child. Apparently, the baby that her daughter was carrying had been fathered by André. What is more, she referred to André as her son-in-law. So obviously, this relationship was more than a casual one.

'Sophia was angry that André had the audacity to formalise a relationship with another woman behind her back. Who would not be, Your Honour? He betrayed her trust. And apparently, it was not the first time he had done this. The defence tells us that he made a habit of having affairs. However, this time Mrs Kruger had had enough. So she planned and plotted and lay in wait for her husband.

'True to form, André arrived home inebriated and unreasonable. This was her opportunity. She began to argue with him and provoke him. When he bent over to vomit, she took her opportunity and beat his head in. Do you blame her? He seemed to be a flawed and difficult person. Sophia was tired of him, tired of his affairs, and tired of his cruelty.

'Apparently, according to the defence, André Kruger was also having sex with his daughters. Regrettably, there is no real evidence to back up this claim. However, let's say that there is some truth in it. I believe this would have further fuelled Mrs Kruger's plan to get rid of her husband.

'The defence put forward the theory that the accused acted in self-defence. Let us examine the legal elements required to establish self-defence. First, was there an imminent threat to her life? Why, on this particular day, was it more dangerous for the accused? Many witnesses have said in these proceedings that the victim made a habit of beating Sophia Kruger. However, none have said that he had ever tried to kill her.

'Second, was there no other option available to the accused but to take the action she did, which resulted in the death of the victim? Did she have to hit him on the head with the malachite lamp? Not really. She could just as easily have escaped through the bedroom door when the accused was vomiting. But she chose not to. Thank you.' Rudo stood up to present her closing arguments. 'Your Honour, I really wish that life and people were as simple as the account Mr Mafuta has just given. Unfortunately, families are not. They are complicated.

'The prosecution's argument is that on the day in question in October, Sophia was very angry. She was angry because she had found out that her husband had had an affair and a child with Ms Ndlovu, who lived up the road at number twenty-eight. So, she planned that when André came home and began to beat her and strangle her with his belt, she would take the opportunity while he was vomiting to pick up the heavy bedside lamp and beat his skull in. The Kruger housekeeper tells us that it was not unusual for Mr Kruger's lady friends to pop up from various places. Sophia was used to his adulterous behaviour. I think that was the least of her problems.

'Let me draw an alternative picture. Your Honour, I promised you a journey that highlights the complexities of human nature. The victim, André Kruger, enjoyed having sex with underage girls. You may think that I am bold to draw such a conclusion. Well, that is the only conclusion I can draw based on the facts presented to me. Sophia Kruger was his first victim – that we know of. She was fourteen years old when a construction worker at her school, André Kruger, began grooming her by paying her attention and making her feel special. She was flattered that this older, powerful man was taking an interest in her. By the age of fifteen, she was a mother and married to her abuser.

'He was already in his late twenties. So this fifteen-year-old girl from a sheltered background with strict Muslim parents moved to a home where her new husband was more controlling than her father. The honeymoon was over very quickly. We heard testimony from Diara Kruger that she could not remember a time during her childhood when her home was free of violence.

'We do not have any information about Mr Kruger's relationships before he met the accused. However, research shows us that men who have sex with children usually begin doing so when they are teenagers. The next time André came to our attention was when the family was flagged by the authorities as being at risk. This was the result of his daughter Diara's attempt to take her own life. André Kruger had been exposed for abusing his two older daughters. We have testimony from the government psychologist to support this. It appears that no girl in the neighbourhood was exempt from his advances. However, nothing about Mr Kruger's behaviour was new to his wife. We have heard testimony from the policeman in charge of the case that, when Mrs Kruger was arrested on the fateful night her husband died, she had been well and truly beaten. We have all seen the pictures of her injuries. Does she look like she lay awake waiting to attack him? No, it looks more like her husband came home angry and ready to take his frustrations out on her. This was hardly a revenge killing, it was pure self-defence.

'Let me summarise André Kruger's behaviour. First, he got drunk whenever possible. Second, he found as many underage girls as possible and forced or lured them into a sexual relationship. Third, when he was at home, he beat his wife as often as he liked, which was often. I think that sums it up. There was nothing new here for Sophia. Just another day. After years and years of being beaten to a pulp by her husband, do you honestly think that she had the courage or strength to stand up to him? I think not. This is a mother who failed to protect her own daughters from sexual abuse. Sophia, like other victims of domestic violence, believed that she was wrong and she "deserved" the abuse. Why would she wait more than twenty-five years before she looked for an opportunity to kill him?

'More plausible to any reasonable person is that it was a terrible accident instigated by André Kruger. Sophia feared for her life. Where else would a woman of Sophia's stature find the strength to hit him on the head to save her life? This was no slow burn. This petite lady was fighting for her life. She must have been terrified. He had her pinned down to the bed, he had slapped her and beaten her with his fists, and now he was strangling her with his belt. Luckily, she was given a reprieve. All the drinking had resulted in

André having to vomit. This gave Sophia the opportunity to grab the object nearest to her, hit him and run. Her intention was only to slow him down so she could save her life. Not kill him. We cannot refute the fact that danger was imminent.

'The medical examiner has testified that André Kruger's death was not caused solely by the blow from the lamp. A major contribution was his falling face down onto the hard floor in the bedroom. So really, the issue of intent appears moot to me. There is no evidence of murderous intent by Sophia. This was an abused woman, who became a teenage mum with a much older husband. She did not have the opportunity to learn good decision-making skills or alternative means of conflict resolution. She had the courage beaten out of her. She did not even have the courage to save her daughter from being raped by her husband.

'The second question that begs to be answered by Your Honour is that of sentencing. Given the dynamics in the Kruger family, was it not likely that this man – this violent, abusive man – would meet a violent end? I ask you, with respect, to recognise the dynamics of this family when making your decision. Please do not think that the violence that these women suffered was a peripheral issue. In fact, it is a very deep and systemic problem. Unfortunately, power and privilege allow most men to go unchallenged. Also, we can see from André Kruger that perpetrators can look "normal".

'So, Your Honour, because you have the power and privilege to do so, I beg you to say that the violent, vicious behaviour that André Kruger and others like him inflict is unacceptable. I ask you respectfully to stand with André Kruger's victims and recognise all the crimes he has committed. Crimes that went unpunished. We cannot be silent and collude with André and ignore his behaviour

– behaviour that almost destroyed his family. Behaviour that resulted in one of his daughters trying to take her own life. You may say that he was the victim in this instance. And he was. The victim of a terrible accident, where his wife feared for her life. This was pure self-defence; Sophia had no intention of causing André harm or of killing him. She was seeking to protect *herself* from imminent harm or death. Mr Kruger's death was the result of his own violent and abusive behaviour. He would not be dead today if he had not come home that night and attempted to strangle his wife. If he had come home that night and gone straight to bed, we would not be here today. Allow me to end, Your Honour, by quoting Martin Luther King: "In the end, we will remember not the words of our enemies, but the silence of our friends."

'Let us not remain mute. Let us break this cycle of violence. Thank you.'

17

JUDGMENT

THE STATE VS SOPHIA KRUGER
(CHANETSA, JUDGE RESIDING)

The judge cleared his throat, then spoke. 'Judgment is handed down in the matter of the State vs Sophia Kruger. The salient facts and decision in this matter are as follows:

'The accused is charged with murder under the Criminal Law (Codification and Reform) Act [Chapter 9:23] in relation to the death of her husband. The accused confessed to accidentally killing her husband, André Kruger. By law, a trial must be conducted to assess the facts and evidence before a conviction can be made.

In this matter, we were required to assess three salient factual and legal questions: one, how credible was the accused's confession that she was responsible for the death of her husband? Was the accused's confession made without any form of intimidation? Two. Has the prosecution proved, beyond reasonable doubt, that the accused had an actual intention to kill? Three, has the defence proved, beyond reasonable doubt, that André Kruger's death was accidental and carried out in self-defence? With respect to question one, no evidence has been produced during this hearing that questions the credibility of the confession made by the accused. I accept the evidence of the housekeeper, who confirmed that if Mr Kruger were engaged in violence against the accused in the bedroom, the door would be locked, making it difficult for anyone to aid her. I also accept that the only other occupants of the house were three of their daughters, who were asleep at the time. I therefore accept the accused's confession as credible and find that the accused was responsible for the death of her husband. There is no evidence of any form of intimidation or duress in obtaining her confession.'

'With respect to question two, the evidence produced by the prosecution does not support a finding of actual intent to commit murder. I accept that the deceased came home inebriated and began to physically abuse the accused. This is supported by pictures of the injuries sustained by the accused. I am satisfied that on the night in question, the accused feared for her life. She was locked in a room with the deceased, with little time to decide on an escape route. I am satisfied that the accused was being subjected to physical violence and may have been in fear of her life at that time. While her actions resulted in the death of her husband, the evidence does not support the allegation that the accused formed an actual intent to kill her husband.

'With respect to question three, the defence is arguing that Mrs Kruger acted in self-defence when she struck the deceased on the head, resulting in his death. I am satisfied that the accused lived in a home where physical violence was the norm. This is corroborated by Diara Kruger, the daughter of the accused, and a psychological evaluation carried out by the expert witness. I agree with the defence that the accused was in fear of her life. She was left with no alternative but to take action to save herself from imminent danger. I did not find evidence that the accused had tried in the past to end her husband's life. Her psychological evaluation clearly states that she blamed her own shortcomings for any physical abuse she suffered at the hands of her husband.

'It is therefore my judgment that the deceased, André Kruger, died as a result of injuries caused by Sophia Kruger in self-defence. I therefore find the accused not guilty. The accused is free to go.'

18

SHAAN

'Shaan, pull yourself together,' Diara snapped. 'Why are you crying? Mum is coming home. She is not guilty!'

They were driving home after the judgment. A verdict of self-defence was what Rudo had hoped for – and what she had achieved. Diara's thoughts went back to the scene in the courtroom: the spectators erupting into joyful clapping and ululating. Rudo turning to make eye contact with her while leaning over to hug her client. Shaan bursting into tears and clutching her, almost painfully. Nameless, faceless people patting them and hugging them.

Diara was driving, as Shaan was too distraught after the sentencing. Her sobbing was affecting Farish, who was in the back with her.

'Shay, please, help me out here. The baby is tired and needs feeding. Just talk to him.' Diara tried to distract her sister by giving her a task. The baby was wailing, and her breasts responded by leaking. Shaan dug around in Farish's nappy bag and found his favourite Winnie the Pooh rattle. She shook it at him and began to chat away comfortingly to him. He grabbed the toy and started to chew it.

'What's going on, Shaan?'

'I'm just so happy that Mum is coming home at last. She wasted a year and a half in that awful prison for a murder she did not commit.'

'I know. It's wonderful!'

'Dee … there's something I have to tell you.'

'Well, let's wait till we get home and I've settled Farish. He won't let us talk.'

'Okay, but I don't want the girls to hear.'

'We'll wait until they're in bed. Also, don't tell them Mum is coming home. Let it be a surprise!'

Rudo had taken Sophia back to the remand prison to complete some paperwork before her release and collect her belongings. Shaan and Diara had wanted to go with them, but Sophia had urged them to take the baby home and wait for her.

Farish made happy, gleeful noises as he banged his toy. This continued until they were nearly home. Diara was taken by surprise when her sister broke the silence.

'Do you ever think about what he used to do to us?'

Diara chewed her lower lip. This was the first time they had spoken about the incest. In the past, they had never discussed their father's behaviour. Maybe because they did not have the strength to talk about it. And they certainly did not have the language to describe or discuss these traumatic events.

'I used to. All the time. I couldn't stop thinking about it. But since he died, I have found that I can go for longer without him entering my mind. Having Farish has also helped.' She waited for Shaan to say something, but she was silent. Diara tried again. 'How has it been with you, Shaan?'

Shaan continued to stare out of the window as she began to talk, almost in a whisper. 'His temper got worse, you know, after you left. He would break stuff in the house and really beat Mum, worse than before. I tried to help her, but he was too strong for us. He would throw us around. But he stopped doing … all the other stuff.' Shaan stopped to pick up Farish's toy, which had fallen out of his hand as sleep overcame him.

'I'm sorry, Shay. I'm sorry that I left you to deal with him alone.'

Shaan carried on talking as if she had not heard her sister. 'He used to say that he couldn't "do it" with me, even if he was desperate, because I was so ugly. That you were the beautiful one. And you really knew how to – you know … do it with him.'

Diara gasped in shock. The audacity of that brute, portraying her as a willing participant. 'He was sick! I hated his guts. I think I wished him dead more often than I breathed. When he finally died, it was such a relief. I could not squeeze out a single tear.'

'I am glad you got away, Dee.' Shaan took a deep breath. She looked at her sister and their eyes met in the rear-view mirror. 'I missed you so much. But you were safe.' She paused. 'I've always wondered what happened that night you took the overdose. I heard you screaming and him shouting. We were in our rooms, terrified. Mum banged on my window. He had shut her out as usual. I sneaked down the passage to open the kitchen door. Then after a while, when we were back in my room, we heard doors banging. Eventually we went to sleep.'

Diara swallowed, and for the second time that week had to pull the ugly memory from the recesses of her mind. Shaan had not attended the trial, so was not aware of the evidence Diara had given. 'He raped me. He held me by the throat and raped me. That night, I felt that if I stayed in that house a minute longer, I was going to go crazy. I didn't know what to do, and I couldn't cope any more.

Mum was no help. She made me so angry, pretending that nothing had happened. She got beaten and just accepted it, expecting us to do the same. I once asked her why he hurt us in our privates and she said he didn't mean to, he was just "fiddling with us". Can you imagine?'

She took a breath, and another, and tried to still her rapidly beating heart. Perspiration had gathered on her nose and upper lip, and she wiped it away. She took the turn off Sherwood Drive that would take them back to their childhood home. Shaan was gazing out of the window again. 'I thought he had killed you. When you didn't wake up the next morning, I was so scared.'

'I know. I'm sorry.' Diara parked by the front door and they got out of the car. Farish woke as his mother lifted him out of the car, and began to complain.

'I am going to feed Farish and the girls should be home soon. Let's distract them from the subject of Mum by saying that Rudo is coming over. We missed the judgment because Farish was screaming. Okay?'

Shaan nodded and they made their way indoors. Amaani was already back from school and in the kitchen eating a sandwich. She jumped up to take the baby, asking anxiously, 'How's Mum? What happened? Will she be back soon?'

'Mum's fine, sweetie. Where's Annie?'

'She's in her room.'

'No, I'm here,' Annie said, walking into the kitchen.

'Hi. How was varsity today?'

Annika was in the second year of her legal degree. She worked part-time at a haberdashery in the nearby Mabelreign shopping centre. Amaani was still at school, in her O level year.

'Come and sit down, girls. Shaan and I didn't make it to the court on time so Rudo is coming to talk to us about how Mum's case ended.'

They all sat down around the dining table in the kitchen as Diara fed her hungry baby. Shaan came in and made tea. Afterwards, the two younger girls played with Farish. Diara did her best to keep the younger ones distracted, but she could see that their thoughts were with their mother. Suddenly Amaani asked out of the blue, 'Dee, if Mum goes to prison will we have to leave this house?'

'No, my darling. Not at all. I spoke to Rudo about that, because the house belonged to Dad. Apparently, according to the law, the house now belongs to Mum because she is his legal wife. It's irrelevant if Mum has committed a crime against Dad. The only way Mum would not inherit the house is if Dad left a will bequeathing it to someone else. We are almost sure that he did not, but Rudo will do a legal search. The will would have had to be lodged with a lawyer and have proper witnesses and stuff like that. Does that make sense?'

Amaani nodded, looking relieved.

'Think about it. If you have any more questions, we will check with Rudo. Okay?' Diara said.

Annika reached over to hold hands with Amaani – a childhood habit that had stuck.

'Maybe, if we all save up, you guys can come to London for a holiday. What do you think?'

The two girls nodded solemnly. But it was too soon. They were still absorbing the information.

It was another hour before there was a hoot at the gate. Diara sent the two younger girls to bring Rudo in. She felt tearful when she heard their cries of delight when they saw Sophia.

'Where's Ambuya?' asked Diara. 'Let's all go out for lunch and we can talk more. How about Nando's?'

Rudo left, and Sophia had a bath and said her prayers. Diara bundled everyone into the car along with Farish, who was delighted at all the attention he was receiving from his aunts and granny.

Diara looked around the table at her family as they talked and played with the baby. This was the first time they had all been out for a meal together. She shook off the thought and vowed that this would be the first of many.

✿✿✿

That night, after Farish was in bed, Diara and Shaan continued their earlier conversation. Shaan had been quiet all afternoon, even at lunch. 'Shay, are you going to be all right?' Diara asked as they sat in the lounge with a cup of tea. Sophia and the girls had gone to bed, Sophia in Diara's room for obvious reasons.

Shaan looked up. 'Ja. I think so. I'll do my best.'

'I know you will. And I'll be there if you need anything. Promise me you will keep going to your sessions with Mandy.'

'Dee, I have to tell you something. Mum made me promise not to tell anyone, but if I don't tell someone I will go crazy. I know I can tell you.'

'What's wrong?'

'It's about the night Dad died.'

Diara felt cold fingers of dread squeeze her heart. 'What about it? What's wrong?'

'I wanted to tell you, but Mum said no. She said that once you tell one person, a secret is not a secret any longer.'

'What secret?'

'About what happened that day. The day that Mum got arrested.' Shay began to gabble. 'It was my Saturday off. I was in the kitchen making toast and Ambuya came in and said there was some woman wanting to see Mum about Dad.'

208

'Where was he?'

'At work. Mum had them brought into the house. It was a lady who worked for the family down the road at number twelve. She was with her daughter, who looked about fifteen. She had a tiny baby tied to her back.'

Diara held her breath. For some reason, she had a strong feeling that this event that Shaan was recounting from the day of the murder was going into new terrain.

'The mother seemed very angry. She said that her daughter was Dad's girlfriend and he had promised to marry her. He had even paid her some *lobola*. I can't remember how much.'

Lobola is the Shona word for 'bride price', paid by the prospective husband in cash or kind to the family of the bride.

'What happened next?' asked Diara, not sure if she wanted to know but not wanting to interrupt. Something was interfering with Shaan's ability to move on with her life.

'Apparently, they had not seen Dad for a long time. He hadn't been to see the baby, who was two months old. She said that she had phoned him many times, but he was ignoring her.'

'What did the daughter say?'

'Nothing. She just stood there. She was younger than Amaani, I think. It was absurd. A child with a child tied on her back.' Shaan stopped and topped up her tea. She did not speak until she was seated again. 'She told us that Dad was her son-in-law and the baby, a boy called Tatenda, was his child. But he was not looking after the child. She said that if he did not want to look after the child, he should pay damages. She also said that two girls on the next street were also claiming that Dad was their boyfriend.'

Diara felt hatred and rage rise in her. 'Bloody bastard! Poor Mum! Having to live with that shit every day. No wonder she lost it that night and killed him.'

In distress, Shaan covered her face. Diara rubbed her arm sympathetically. Her mind was consumed by disgust with her father, and she was totally unprepared when her sister said, 'It wasn't her, Dee. I hit him on the head.'

'What?'

'I wanted to tell you, but Mum wouldn't let me.'

Diara scooted over to her sister. 'Oh God, Shaan. What happened?'

'It was a mistake. I didn't mean to. It just happened.' She wrung her hands.

'Of course you didn't mean it! And even if you did, good on you. I am the last person on earth to judge you. I wished him dead so often. Come on. Tell me what happened.'

'When Dad got home from work at lunchtime, Mum told him about the visit from his "wife" and "mother-in-law". He called Mum a "fucking lying bitch" and stormed off. He returned later that night and began beating her – and I went in. He had his belt around Mum's throat and was strangling her. Her face was bright red and her eyes were popping out.' Shaan was speaking in a monotone and staring off into the distance.

'I ran in, picked up the lamp, stood on the bed, and hit him as hard as I could. It never occurred to me that he would die. I just wanted to save Mum.'

'So, he wasn't bending down to vomit?'

'No, he had already done that. When I hit him, he fell forward, into the vomit. His head began to bleed. He twitched a couple of times but didn't move.'

'And Mum?'

'I got her some water. After a few minutes, she stopped

gasping and could breathe. Her nose was bleeding, and she was having difficulty swallowing.' She shrugged. 'Mum and I didn't realise he was dead for a while. Mum went over to him, and by this time there was a puddle of blood round his head. She checked his pulse, couldn't find one. I started to panic. But she was very calm. She told me to say nothing, that she would talk to the police.' Shaan looked at her sister and smiled sadly. 'Before I knew what was happening, she was arrested and taken away. I didn't know what to do.'

'I know. I know. It's okay.'

'I don't care that I killed him. I only care that Mum went to jail for something I did.' There was so much remorse in her voice that Diara felt a physical ache in her heart. No wonder her sister was struggling emotionally.

'Look, Shay, Mum made that choice to save you. To save all of us. She finally stood up for us.'

When her sister remained quiet, Diara spoke again. She hoped her words were comforting. 'You got rid of our nightmare and she took the blame. But *you* saved our family. Maybe Mum felt that she should take the blame since she had failed to protect us from him when he was alive. I don't know.'

Shaan nodded.

'Do you feel guilty that you killed him?'

'No!' Shaan responded strongly. 'He took our childhood.'

'Yes, he did.' Diara sighed. 'Let's just get on with our lives. Let's try to be a family. He took that from us. But we have the chance to be a new family now.'

'Ja, I guess so.'

Diara moved closer to her sister and held her hands. 'Let's agree to do some things. First, let's stop blaming ourselves for what happened. We had no control over any of it. We have to look forward so that we can live the life we dream of living. Also, let's leave the past behind. It's the past. If we live with anger and hatred, we will block the way for beautiful things to come into our lives. Do you agree?'

Shaan nodded shakily.

'We're gonna be okay,' Diara said, hugging her sister.

'I hope so.'

'There's something else I need to tell you,' Shaan said abruptly, looking at her sister uneasily.

Again, Diara felt nervous about what was to come.

'I have met someone. Someone who is very dear to me. Our relationship has grown, and it is important to me.'

Diara could not hide her relief and delight at the news. 'Wow, really? How fabulous! I am so glad. Tell me more. Where did you meet him?'

Shaan hesitated. 'Her. Her name is Victoria.'

Diara was stunned into silence. Shaan was not making eye contact with her, and Diara realised that her sister was probably misconstruing her silence for judgement. She leant over and hugged her sister tightly. 'That's wonderful, Shaan. I am so glad that you are happy. When do I get to meet Victoria?'

'Really? I'd love for you to meet her. But never call her Vicky or any shortened version of her name. She hates that.'

Diara smiled, then brought up the issue that was worrying her. 'You do realise, sweetie, that here in Zim your relationship with Victoria is illegal, even though you're both consenting adults. You will be careful?'

'I know, but I love her. And I don't think that I can have sex with a man. I tried a couple of times, but I felt terrible afterwards. Once, I just couldn't go through with it.' She was wringing her hands.

'Why? Did something happen?' Diara held her hands and waited for Shaan to compose herself.

'No, no, they were nice, but I just couldn't. I wanted to ask you if the same thing happens to you.'

'Okay.'

'When I am with a man – any man – when I close my eyes, I'm immediately with Dad, and he's doing those things to us. I can't see the face of the man I'm with because, everywhere I look, I see Dad. It's worse if the man has drunk any alcohol. Do you remember how Dad breathed alcohol fumes all over us? It still makes my skin crawl when I smell alcohol.' She covered her face with her hands and sobbed while Diara held her close.

'It's okay, Shaan. It will be okay,' she soothed her sister, knowing how trite it sounded. Her heart was full of anger. *Bastard! Bastard! Would Shaan ever be free?* Shaan stopped weeping. 'But when I'm with Victoria, I don't think of him. I know who I'm with and it feels totally different. I don't feel guilty or dirty.'

'Well then, that's where you should be if that's what makes you happy. Don't try to do something just because everyone else is.'

'Do you feel the same about sex?'

Diara knew she had to choose her words carefully, so that she didn't make her sister feel any worse. 'I don't know. I have only ever been with Alexander, and I have known him for years and cared for him as long. I don't think I have had the same experiences with men as you.'

'I guess so.'

'If someone is right for you, you forget all the nonsense in your life and feel safe with them. Is that how you feel with Victoria?'

A small smile broke out on Shaan's face and she nodded.

'Good, but please be careful. Keep your relationship private. And there is a plus side to this – at least Mum won't ask you if Victoria is circumcised!'

This had the desired effect. Diara told Shaan how, when she had told her mother that she had had a baby, her mother's response had surprised her. 'She said, "Diara, I hope the man was circumcised? The Prophet Muhammad stated that it is a law for men."' Diara imitated her mother's South African accent. The sisters squealed with laughter.

'How ridiculous,' said Shaan. 'But she wasn't bothered that her husband wasn't circumcised?'

That dampened their mirth.

Finally, Shaan broke the silence. 'How much longer will you stay?'

'Another week or so. I need to get all the paperwork together to give to Rudo. She said that someone at her firm would deal with Dad's estate. Then the house can be passed to Mum and she can decide if she wants to stay here, sell it or move to a flat. But that's all for later.'

Diara was worried about the burden of guilt that Shaan was carrying. 'Have you spoken to Mandy about what you told me tonight?'

'No. Not yet. And I don't know if I want to. I wanted to tell you, and I am so glad I did. I feel so much better.'

'That's fine. I just don't want you feeling guilty. Mum made a choice. Please remember that.' She got up. 'I'm exhausted, and Farish will be up soon. I'm going to bed.'

'Dee?' Shaan said suddenly, as if she had just remembered something. 'If you have only ever been with Alexander, he must be Farish's dad.'

'Yes.'

'I thought so!' she exclaimed, clapping her hands. 'I know you told me when you were pregnant that the father was your friend. They have the same eyes.'

'They do,' Diara said, smiling.

'So? Are you close? What's happening?'

They were just sisters again, talking about things that sisters talk about. Boys, babies, marriage.

'Nothing. He has a wife.'

'Oh God!' Shaan was deflated.

'I know. Don't they all?'

'Did you know about his wife?'

'I did. But I just couldn't help myself. When I found I was pregnant, I thought I would have an abortion, but that was easier said than done. It's all so complicated. Let's talk more tomorrow.'

They were saved from further conversation by Farish waking and crying.

19

LONDON, 2010

Diara returned to London, and again her life was filled with work, Farish and keeping in touch with her family in Zimbabwe. She had noticed that her mother was much calmer. Their conversations were always happy. They talked about Farish. In prison, the other women had taught Sophia to knit, so she was now knitting him a sweater.

Shaan told Diara that Sophia did not sleep in the room where André had died. She slept in Diara's bedroom and was slowly learning not to be afraid anymore. She had even contacted her family in Cape Town. She still suffered from migraines, but at least now she was able to visit a doctor and take medication for them.

Shaan had good days and bad days. She still felt so much trauma and guilt, although her counselling sessions with Mandy had helped her to have more good days. However, Diara realised that it would be a while before Shaan would be strong emotionally. If ever. No one knew better than she did how challenging it could be to let go of pain, suffering or fear. Victoria remained an important part of Shaan's life and had a calming influence on her.

Sophia's attitude did not help. After her release, Diara wanted to talk candidly about what had happened the night

André died. She had assumed that Sophia would reassure Shaan that it had been an accident, that she did not blame her. Diara hoped her mother's words would help Shaan to heal. But it did not play out quite like that.

Sophia did not want to talk about her husband's death.

'Mum, Shaan feels bad that you took the blame for Dad's death and spent time in prison instead of her.'

Sophia cut her off. 'Diara!' She held up her hand. 'I am not sure what's got into you. But you have always come up with strange stories.' Her expression was deadpan, not a glimmer of emotion on her face. She turned to Shaan. 'Thank you for trying to make me feel better by taking the blame, but I killed your father. A fact is a fact.'

The sisters stared at her, lost for words. Diara realised that Sophia was not going to discuss the matter. When Shaan tried to protest, Diara squeezed her arm tightly and shook her head. There was no point in pursuing the conversation. It was difficult to understand how her mother's mind worked. She had always been a closed book.

'Mum, why did you never do anything about Dad's abuse of you? Why did you not tell the police?'

Sophia looked startled at Diara's question. She looked down and fiddled with her prayer beads. Finally, as the girls were about to give up, she answered. 'In the beginning, it did not happen so often, and in between he was so good to me that I kept hoping and hoping that he would not do it again. I wanted him to be the man I married. That man was so lovely.' Sophia looked tearful. 'But I never saw that man again. He just drank more and his behaviour became worse. I did not know who to tell. I was so scared of him.' Sophia looked lost in thought. 'I think something went wrong in André's family. I never met his family and he never spoke about them. I asked once, and he walked away.

But someone called Joshua haunted him – he would wake up at night shouting his name.'

Diara wondered if her father had beaten every emotion out of Sophia. Since primary school, she had watched her mother withdraw more and more. She would either be suffering a migraine, locked in her room, or just silent. Apart from her family, she had no one to talk to. André did not encourage any of them to have friends.

Perhaps this had been Sophia's coping strategy: to become an empty shell of a human being. Feeling was too difficult. Did she feel that she should be punished by being in jail, because she had failed to protect her children? Or had she convinced herself that she had actually killed André? Was killing him an ongoing fantasy that Shaan had helped her realise? She had a history of denying reality, after all – to this day, she denied that the incest had ever happened.

Diara tried to recall times when Sophia had behaved like a 'normal' mum, but it was so hard. Perhaps, with time, she would remember how to behave normally. There were already signs of this in her behaviour with Farish. The two younger girls were overjoyed to have her home, and she responded to them as she did to Farish. But she was less comfortable with Diara and Shaan. Why? Was it down to guilt?

❁❁❁

Xander, true to his word, sent money directly to Farish's account, kept in touch frequently by email, and called monthly. Their conversations usually focused on the baby, his progress and his needs. Diara often wondered what was going on in his life. Had he told Saskia about Farish? Even Leanne didn't know. Neither wanted to pry.

Seven months after the trial, he emailed her. This email

was not his usual one, seeking information about Farish's well-being.

Hi Diara,

Hope you and Farish are well. I'm thinking of coming up to see him for a few days. Is this a convenient time for you? I have attached a copy of my proposed itinerary. Let me know. I've booked to stay at a hotel which is close to your place. I don't want to upset his routine, but could I look after him while I'm around instead of him going to nursery? It would give us a chance to get to know each other.

Xander

Oh God! she thought. *What shall I do? Shall I have him to stay at ours? He should stay with us. He is Farish's dad. He could stay in my room and I could sleep with the baby. But – no! What if he thinks I'm after his body again? How mortifying!*

She rang Leanne for her opinion. In her no-nonsense way, Leanne told her not to be ridiculous. Of course he wanted to stay with them – that was why he had mentioned his hotel.

Why did I bother to call her? thought Diara, putting the phone down. She was not convinced by Leanne's words. To her mind, Xander was only saying, 'I'm coming to see my boy, so let me spend time with him while you are at work.'

Finally, she gave up trying to analyse what he meant. If he wanted to stay with her, he should jolly well say so. In the end she emailed back.

Hey Xander!

Of course. That would be lovely. Farish will love it. But let me warn you: he's exhausting now that he's running around! So be prepared. Come over whenever you want to – I will be home all day on the day you arrive. This will give you two the opportunity to get used to each other, and we can go through his routine together.

See you soon. Sending you love,

Diara and Farish

❁❁❁

Xander arrived just before lunch, as she was preparing to feed Farish before putting him down for his nap. Xander was extremely disappointed when the baby screamed at the sight of him. Farish was hungry, tired and grumpy, and not willing to be parted from his mother, despite all the new toys that Xander had brought him.

'He's forgotten me!' Openly distressed, Xander kept looking at Farish. 'I left it too long to see him again.'

Diara felt bad for him. 'Give him time, Xander. He's just tired. Come into the kitchen and help distract him while I feed him.'

As Farish ate, he was more willing to play with the stranger in his home. But not for long. Once he'd had enough to eat, he was ready for his afternoon nap. Diara took him through to his room to breastfeed him and put him down. After his nap, he was more willing to interact with his father, and enjoyed playing with him. Xander bathed him, and Diara smiled when she heard her son giggling at Xander. The next day when Xander arrived in the morning, Farish was pleased to see him. They established a routine whereby Xander would arrive in the morning and spend the day with his son while Diara was at work. By the time she returned, Farish was fed and bathed and they played for a while before he fell asleep. Evenings were usually spent with Leanne and Aidan. Either they would come over or Xander would go to them after Farish was in bed. The friendship continued as if nothing was amiss. Two couples, one with a baby, spending time together. It felt as if this had always been their routine. Aidan and Leanne asked after Saskia and Xander assured them she was fine. Diara felt his eyes on her, but she refused to make eye contact.

On Friday evening, after Xander had been with them almost a week, he surprised her by saying, 'I wondered if you would be willing to bring the baby and come over to visit me in Jo'burg.'

They were sitting at the kitchen table, eating pasta. Leanne and Aidan were out for the evening, so they were on their own. Diara made no attempt to hide her surprise. Since he had opened the door, she asked the million-dollar question. 'How would Saskia feel about that?'

He looked at her. 'I don't know. She left me.'

'Left? What do you mean, left?'

'I told her about the baby as soon as I got back to Jo'burg after seeing you in Zim. She was angry. She left the next day to stay with her parents in Cape Town.'

'Oh no! That's not good.' She felt sick. She put down her fork and took a sip of water. She waited for him to say more, but when he remained silent, she said what she was thinking. 'I'm so sorry, Xander. I've made a mess of everything.'

He continued talking, as if he had not heard her. 'I tried calling her so many times, and after a month I went over to talk to her. But she was adamant that she wasn't coming back. A month later she sent me divorce papers, citing my adultery.'

She listened in shocked silence, not sure what to say. Shame crept over her.

'That's why it's taken me so long to come over to see you and the baby.' He looked up from his food. 'It's okay, Diara. I'm all right now. She was truly angry and sad about the miscarriages. No matter how much therapy she had or how much we talked about everything, she was still angry. I think she didn't want to be married to me any longer. What happened between you and me was just an excuse.'

'And you? Did you want to continue being married to her?'

He thought about it for a long time before he answered. 'Honestly, I don't know. It just got too hard to remain with her. I tried to give her as much support as I could, but it never seemed enough.' He looked straight at her. 'I thought we cared enough for each other to overcome the challenges, but each time one issue was dealt with, a new one would emerge.' He shook his head. 'Maybe I was doing something wrong. I'm not sure. I'm tired of trying to understand why it all happened.'

'But Xander, why was her adultery forgivable and not yours? Surely, since you had both "sinned", you could move forward from that?'

He sighed. 'I know. I thought the same. We talked about it with our counsellor after Saskia left me. She told us that we had both messed up by not telling the other immediately that we'd been unfaithful. She also explained that the only person who can decide what constitutes being unfaithful is the wounded party.' Xander shrugged. 'I had forgiven Saskia for being unfaithful – I knew she was hurting, and she was punishing both of us by having an affair with Cecil. I don't think she would have done it normally ... Things had been going wrong for a long time before Farish arrived. In all honesty, I think that when we met in Jo'burg, things were already so difficult between Saskia and me that seeing you again brought back the feelings I've always had for you.'

'I suppose so, but I hated the fact that we were sort of shoving it in her face. You know, the baby thing. It felt so cruel.'

They fell silent and resumed eating. Farish stirred, and Diara left to check on him. She still breastfed him at night, so he was probably ready for a feed. She picked him up, soothed him and sat down on the rocking chair to feed him. Xander came in after a while and sat on the carpet next to her. He stroked Farish's hair back off his forehead, watching him feed. Diara picked up the conversation that the baby had interrupted. 'Is there any hope that the two of you will reconcile?'

'No. She has made that crystal clear.'

They were silent again.

'I love watching you feed him.'

Startled by this admission, Diara looked at him. He was looking straight at her, as if waiting for her to respond. She looked away quickly and he sighed. Diara was not sure what to say. The atmosphere in the room had changed; she felt a mixture of discomfort and pleasure. She always felt discomfort when she thought of herself as a sexual being, with needs and desires.

Thanks, Dad, she thought with some bitterness. Then she immediately hated herself for regressing like that. *Stop it! That's all behind you. There is no one left who can come between you and the life you want. Only yourself.* Immediately, pleasure stole over her. He loved to watch her! Or was he watching the baby? She was still trying to resolve her thoughts when Xander spoke again.

'I had better get going,' he said quietly. 'It's late, and you must be tired.'

She stopped him by putting out her hand and touching his arm. 'Can you stay a while? It's Friday, so I'm home tomorrow.'

'Are you sure?'

She nodded.

'Okay. Let me put the kettle on.'

Diara put the baby down in his cot and rubbed his back soothingly till he settled down. She leant down to kiss him and felt an overwhelming wave of affection. He really was beautiful.

Xander had made coffee and taken it through to the lounge. She sat down next to him on the sofa, then broached the subject that had worried her for a while. 'I was thinking … since you only have a few days left before you go back, maybe you'd like to stay with us.'

She waited for him to respond.

'You could have my room and I could sleep with the baby,' she added quickly.

'Or I could sleep with him?' he said.

Diara chuckled in relief. 'You're too big for the little bed in his room. Also, I would still have to wake up to feed him. So, check out and bring your bag over in the morning. And when would you like us to come over to you?' It would just add a small detour to her original plan to visit her family in Zimbabwe.

Xander smiled. 'Tell me when it's convenient for you.'

'Let me check my schedule. Maybe I can go to Zim from there and visit Mum and the girls.'

'I could come with you to Zim.'

'You don't have to.'

'I want to.' He hesitated, then looked as if he had decided on something. 'Diara, I thought we could talk about some plans concerning the baby.'

'Okay,' she said, not liking the sound of that.

'I have been thinking for a while that we should talk about our relationship. I don't believe that Farish was the result of a random one-night stand. I know that I think of

224

you two being in my life. I can't imagine just being Farish's dad for a few months a year. Or being his dad without you there. You once said that I was important to you. Does that still apply? Or have I blown it?' He laughed self-consciously.

Diara looked at him, confused. 'That will never change, Xander. Even more so now because of Farish. We have to be in each other's lives for ever because of him.'

'Would you consider us being more than friends who had a baby together?' Xander asked.

Diara digested his words. *What does he mean? Does he only want us to be together because of Farish? What will happen if the relationship doesn't work? I don't want to lose him as a friend.* She voiced her concerns to him.

'Listen, Dee. This is how I see it. We have been friends for a long time. You know me. I know you. There has always been an attraction between us which we never explored because you had your reasons, and I took the easy route. But we can now.' He stopped and looked at her for a response. When none was forthcoming, he continued.

'I don't want you to be with me just because of the baby. Whatever you decide, I will do my best for you both. I want you to decide if *you* want to be with me.' He moved closer to her and took her hand.

She felt under pressure to respond. She stood up and sat down again, feeling cornered. He quickly added, 'Unless I'm wrong about how you feel?'

'No,' she mumbled. 'You're not wrong.'

Xander lifted her hand and kissed her palm. Diara felt a burst of affection for him. He was so good. So kind. He always said the right thing.

He leant over and kissed her on her mouth. She responded eagerly. She had misssed him, and quickly got lost in his embrace. His familiar smell and feel were comforting, as always. Their passion escalated and she somehow found herself in his lap, straining to get closer to him. Xander picked her up and was making his way towards her bedroom when she had a reality check. Her mind started buzzing. She wanted him so much. She couldn't believe that Xander wanted to build a life with her. What if things went wrong?

He put her down near her bed and leant down to kiss her again, holding her close.

Diara put her fingers on his mouth to stop him. 'Wait, Xan. Please.'

He looked at her inquiringly as he continued to rub her back soothingly. 'It's fine, Dee, we can take it as slow as you like. No hurry. You tell me what you want to do.'

Oh God, she thought. *He is so attentive. So perfect.* Xander held her close, leaning down so his chin rested on her head. She battled with words in her head. How could she explain how she felt? She looked up at him and spoke softly. 'You know, better than anyone, what kind of childhood I had. I know it's in the past, and I really don't want it to affect the rest of my life. But my problem is trust. I find it so hard to trust anyone. And I don't want my insecurities to destroy us.'

Xander did not respond. He just continued to stroke her hair as she spoke.

'I don't know if I believe in monogamy. I think that evolution explains it well. Men are programmed to have lots of sexual partners. That's how they keep the species going. The two of us are perfect examples. Look what we did to Saskia. I don't think I'm capable of having a relationship.'

Xander sat down on the bed and pulled her with him. She stopped talking as she felt tears threatening. He lifted her chin up and smiled at her. She dared to look at him.

'I disagree, Diara. You have so many relationships with other people – Leanne, your sisters.'

'But I haven't had one with a man!' she exclaimed before she could stop herself. It sounded so lame to her ears, but it was a real fear. It was the first time she had said it aloud. 'Please don't pressure me. Don't take me on for Farish's sake. It will not go well.' She was wringing her hands, avoiding eye contact. His determination grew but he remained silent. He knew she was trying to keep her distance from him. Leanne had warned him that she would push him away, and he was ready for that.

'I know. And I really like the fact that you're even considering having a relationship with me. I understand your issues about trusting me, and you're right. I think you are trying to say that you're afraid that I will be unfaithful to you too. Yes?'

She nodded, feeling more miserable now that he had voiced it.

'All I can say is, you know that it's not in my nature to cheat usually. Can you remember if I cheated on any of my girlfriends at varsity?'

'No, I suppose not.'

'So please don't think of me like that. You may as well rip my heart out.' Xander leant down and kissed her gently on the lips. She pulled away, stood up and moved away from him.

'Try to understand, please. Sometimes I feel like I live in a black swamp, and you don't belong there. I won't pull you down there with me. You need to be here, in the light, for Farish. He needs you. But I have so many wounds. Can't you see that?'

Xander made no move to comfort her. He thought back to what Leanne had said to him when they'd discussed his long-term plans. *She is so lonely, Xander. Imagine a loneliness where you forget how to talk, forget how to express your feelings.*

He pulled his thoughts together. 'I remember the first time I saw you. We were registering for our first year in the great hall at varsity. You were standing in the queue next to me, clutching your clipboard. I couldn't see your face, just your profile. So I waited and waited for you to turn round.' He smiled as he remembered the day. 'You were wearing that red checked shirt, and sneakers. Your hair was so shiny, so black, and covered your back like a waterfall. You had pushed it back behind one ear and you wore a tiny giraffe earring. You would look down and your hair would fall forward, and you would push it back again behind your ear. At one stage, it was really annoying you, so you grabbed it and twisted it round your hand.' Xander took a sip of his cold coffee and grimaced. 'Then, when I had given up hope that you would ever turn round, Leanne called your name and you turned. Your hair swung over your shoulder and you hugged each other. I finally saw your face. The heat in the hall had smudged your eyeliner. I was fascinated by you. You looked fragile and wounded. But you smiled, and it was like the softest touch. I wanted to feel that touch pass over me. I wanted that touch to be just for me.'

He stopped and ran his fingers through his hair, still not looking at her. 'And did I deserve that touch? No, because I didn't have the balls to ask you for it. I didn't have the balls to help you open your wounds and lick them. I have carried that regret with me for so long. I blame myself for being so pathetic. Do you remember when it was Leanne's birthday one year – I think it was our second year – and everyone pressured you to try weed? Do you remember?' He grinned and ran his hand through his hair. She gave no response, so he continued. 'You only had a few puffs and then sat quietly with a pained look on your face. Then I was on the way to the loo and I saw you in the passage, leaning against the wall and clutching your head with both hands, your eyes shut. When I asked if you were all right or wanted help, you whispered for me to help you to your room as you had to lie down. You tried to walk towards your room but it was difficult as you kept stopping and moaning, as if you were in pain. I finally had to carry you. Do you remember?'

'Vaguely.'

'Well, your hair smelt of apples. We got to your room and I put you down, and you sat on the floor, holding your head. I lifted you onto the bed and you curled up in a foetal position. I covered you and turned to leave, then you said, "Please don't leave me. There are ping-pong balls jumping up and down in my head."' He squeezed her tighter. 'You were so adorable. So confused. I think it was the first time you had ever asked me for help. You were usually like a wounded animal, biting anyone who held their hand out to help you. And I didn't have the emotional intelligence to help you. But you know what? I often imagined that I was with you when I was with other women – nameless, faceless people I can't even remember now. How pathetic is that? Almost perverted.'

Diara was angry. She walked back towards him, her fists clenched tightly at her side. 'Then why did you marry Saskia, if you felt that way about me? How could you? Do you know how that made me feel? I was devastated. She was so different from me. So perfect and so white – everything that I was not. I was just a coloured girl from the wrong side of the railway track. Good enough for a good time but not good enough for forever.'

'You have every right to think that. But I'm asking you to try to forgive me. Forgive me for being a coward. Forgive me for taking the easy way out and not fighting for you. I'm ashamed that I behaved like a bigot and gave in to my parents' belief that white is right.'

Diara felt herself softening towards him. She knew she hadn't made it easy for him to approach her. For anyone. 'Listen, we were all victims of racism. Don't blame yourself for all of it. We lived in a country that was notorious for its segregation policies. It's okay, Xander. Our situation is more complicated than the race issue. I have so much baggage and pain. I don't know how to move on. I'm worried that I will harm you with my pain. I only have the strength to look after our boy – and I need you to help me with that. I can't do it on my own. I have my sisters and my mum to think of as well.' Diara finally looked at him. 'Shall we just keep things simple?'

But this time Xander was not caught unawares. He had anticipated this response. He moved closer to her and held her chin up. 'Please, Diara. I understand that you're afraid but could you think about how you said you feel about me? Isn't that a good start? Please don't go silent. Tell me how you feel.'

But she remained silent, waiting for his next sentence. Her heart was pounding.

'To me, you are the most beautiful person I've ever met. I don't want to lose you. I can't bear to be parted from you any longer. It's torture.'

Those were the most wonderful words she had ever heard. Tears overwhelmed her, but for a different reason.

'I don't want you to run away again. You say that don't understand your pain. So, share it with me so that can understand it. Let me listen to your pain. It's the only way we can move on.'

Diara was sobbing. She tried to push him away. Xander however, was not willing to let go. He held her tightly until

230

she was quieter. She moved away and said, her voice sad and subdued, 'Xander, life has made me so ugly. Look at me. I'm a mess.'

'You have just been looking in the wrong mirror. Look at me from now on, and you will never see ugly. My mirror will show you how beautiful you are. I am so lucky to have met you.'

That drew a reluctant smile from her.

'So, what do you say? Do you think we can give us a go? I also put our time together away and took it out whenever I felt down.'

Diara smiled, remembering that she had said those words to him once. 'I'm afraid that my issues will be too much for you to cope with. What if things go wrong between us? I don't want Farish to suffer if we split up.'

But Xander was not to be deterred. He had come prepared with ammunition from Leanne. *She will try to put you off, but you have to keep going. Make it clear that you're not going to go away. Her feelings for you are very strong but she's afraid of getting hurt. You need to tell her why you want to be with her.* That had been Leanne's last piece of advice.

'I'm sorry, Dee. I am not willing to accept that as a reason. How will we know until we try? Are you really going to turn your back on your feelings for me? At least let's give it a go. I don't believe in what-ifs. We are two adults who feel something for each other. We have a son together. What else do we need? I think that's a good starting point.' When she remained silent, he added, 'I have never felt for anyone else what I feel for you, Dee. Believe me, I have been battling it for years. So, what do you think? Can we give it a go?'

Diara felt drained emotionally. She leant against him. *It would be so good to have him around more often, she thought.* She was tired of keeping him at arm's length to protect herself. She was only deluding herself, no one else.

Was she doing what Sophia always did? Protecting herself emotionally by not getting involved?

'Shall we take it slowly and see how we get along?' she asked. 'I can't promise anything, but I will give it my best shot.'

'That's all I want.' He cupped her face with his hands and leant over to kiss her again. 'Now I really need you to kiss me like you mean it. I'm tired of watching you and wanting you. Let's put all the other stuff behind us – Saskia, your dad, all of it. This is our time now. Yours and mine. And we have waited so long for it.'

Diara waited for the familiar feelings of anxiety to bubble up, but they didn't. Then she realised that she was okay. She was all right. What he was suggesting seemed to be sitting well with her. *There are bound to be obstacles*, she thought. *Everyone has those. Maybe we can help each other get past them.* She reached up, stroked the cleft in his chin and smiled.

'I still see the sun on your back, Xander. You've just made it warmer and brighter.'

Printed in Great Britain
by Amazon

20992478R00140